COMPLETE BOOK OF

Grade K

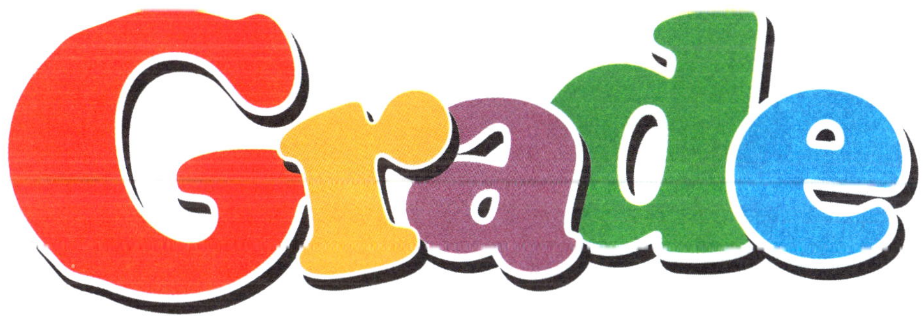

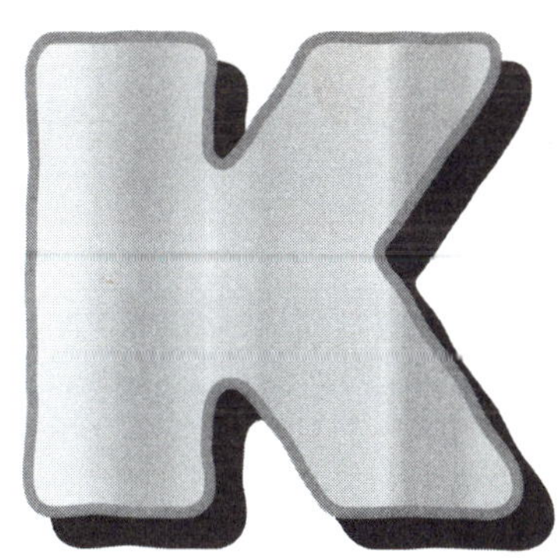

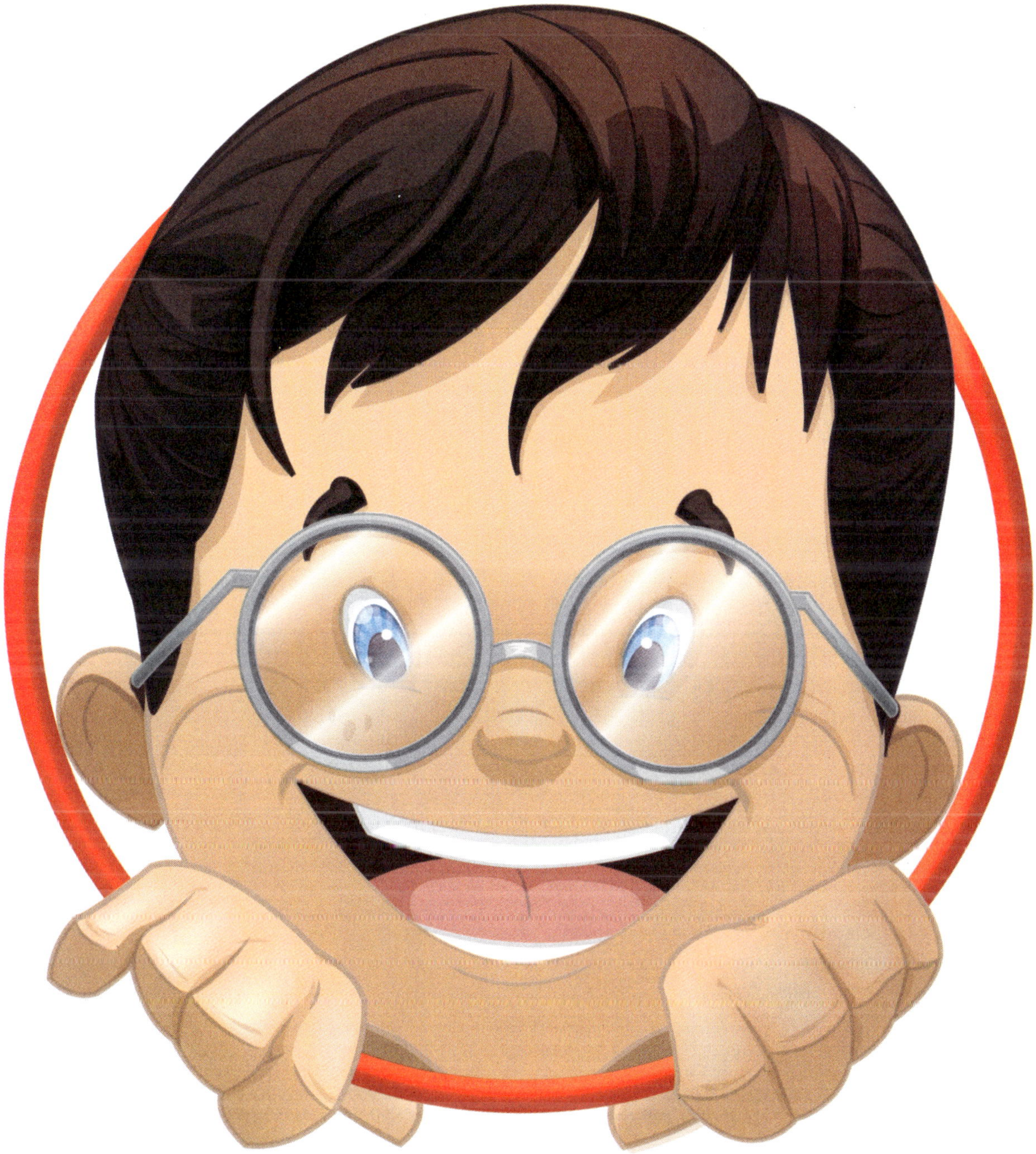

AMERICAN EDUCATION PUBLISHING™

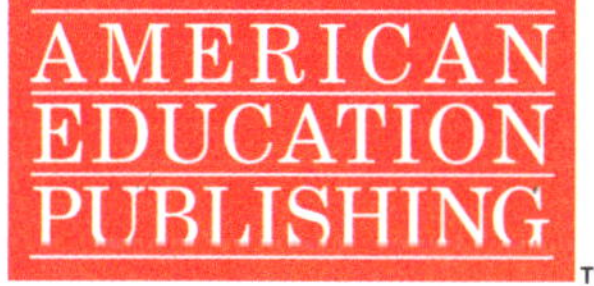

An imprint of Carson-Dellosa Publishing LLC
Greensboro, North Carolina

American Education Publishing™
An imprint of Carson-Dellosa Publishing LLC
P.O. Box 35665
Greensboro, NC 27425 USA

 ISBN 978-0-7696-8580-9
Printed in the USA

07-154137811

Dear Parents, Caregivers, and Educators,

The *Complete Book* series provides young learners an exciting and dynamic way to learn the basic skills essential to learning success. This vivid workbook will guide your student step-by-step through a variety of engaging and developmentally appropriate activities in basic concepts, reading, math, language arts, writing, and fine motor skills.

The *Complete Book of Kindergarten* is designed to be used with an adult's support. Your student will gain the most when you work together through the activities. Below are a few suggestions to help make the most of your learning time together:

- Read the directions aloud. Move your finger under the words as your child watches. As you come to words he or she recognizes, encourage your student to read along.
- Explain the activities in terms your student understands. Talk about the pictures and activities. These conversations will both strengthen your student's confidence and build important language skills.
- Provide support and encouragement to your student. Work with your student at a pace that is comfortable for him or her. End your learning time when your student shows signs of tiring.

To find other learning materials that will interest your young learner and encourage school success, visit www.carsondellosa.com

Table of Contents

Basic Skills

Red Ahead!

Color each picture **red**. Then, draw a picture of something else **red**.

Go, Go Yellow!

Color each picture **yellow**. Then, draw a picture of something else **yellow**.

What's New, Blue?

Circle the **blue** picture in each row.

Going Green

Color each picture **green**. Then, draw a picture of something else **green**.

A Slice of Orange

Circle the **orange** picture in each row.

Purple on Parade

Color each picture **purple**. Then, draw a picture of something else **purple**.

Back to Black

Circle the **black** picture in each row.

Brown All Around

Circle the **brown** picture in each row.

Review Colors

Color the picture.

Review Colors

Color the fruits and vegetables.

Going in Circles

Trace the **circle** below. Then, draw a line under the **circle** in each row.

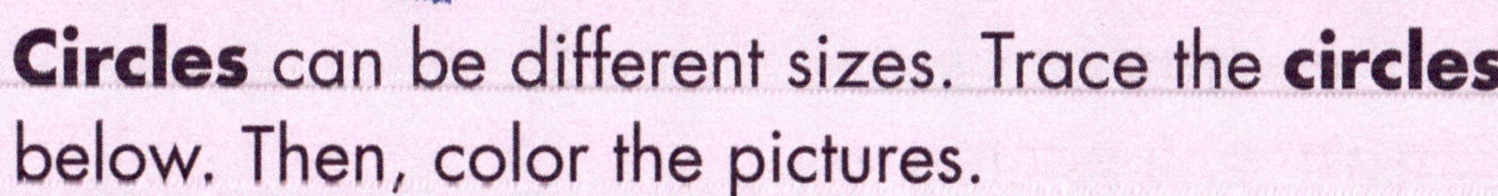

Circles can be different sizes. Trace the **circles** below. Then, color the pictures.

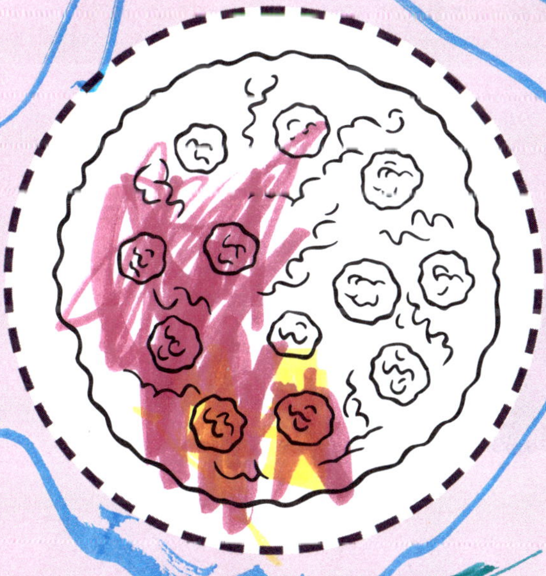

Square Dance

Trace the **square** below. Then, draw a line under the **square** in each row.

Squares have 4 sides of the same length. Help Sue get home. Color the path that has only **squares**.

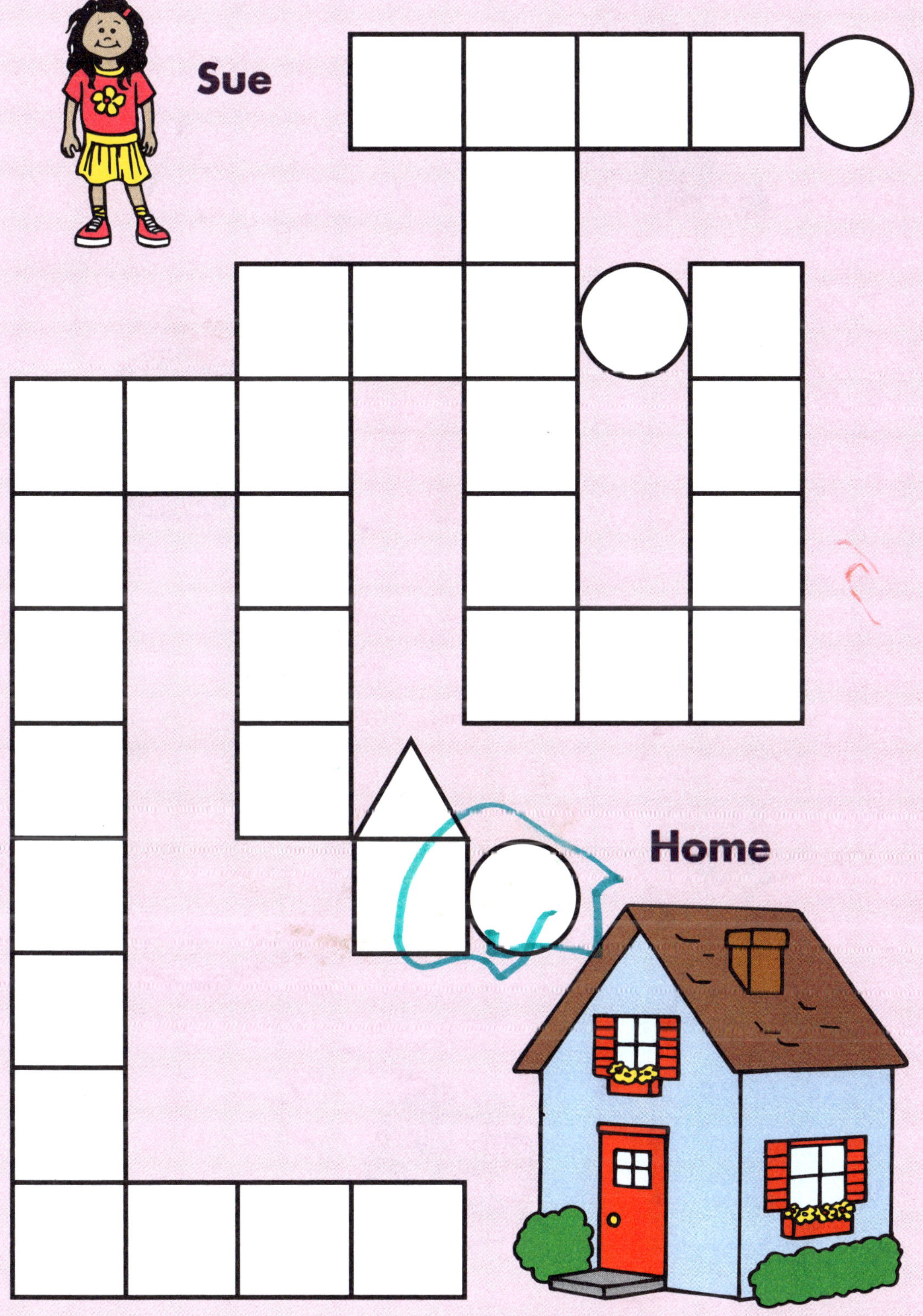

Triangle Time

Trace the **triangle** below. Then, draw a line under the **triangle** in each row.

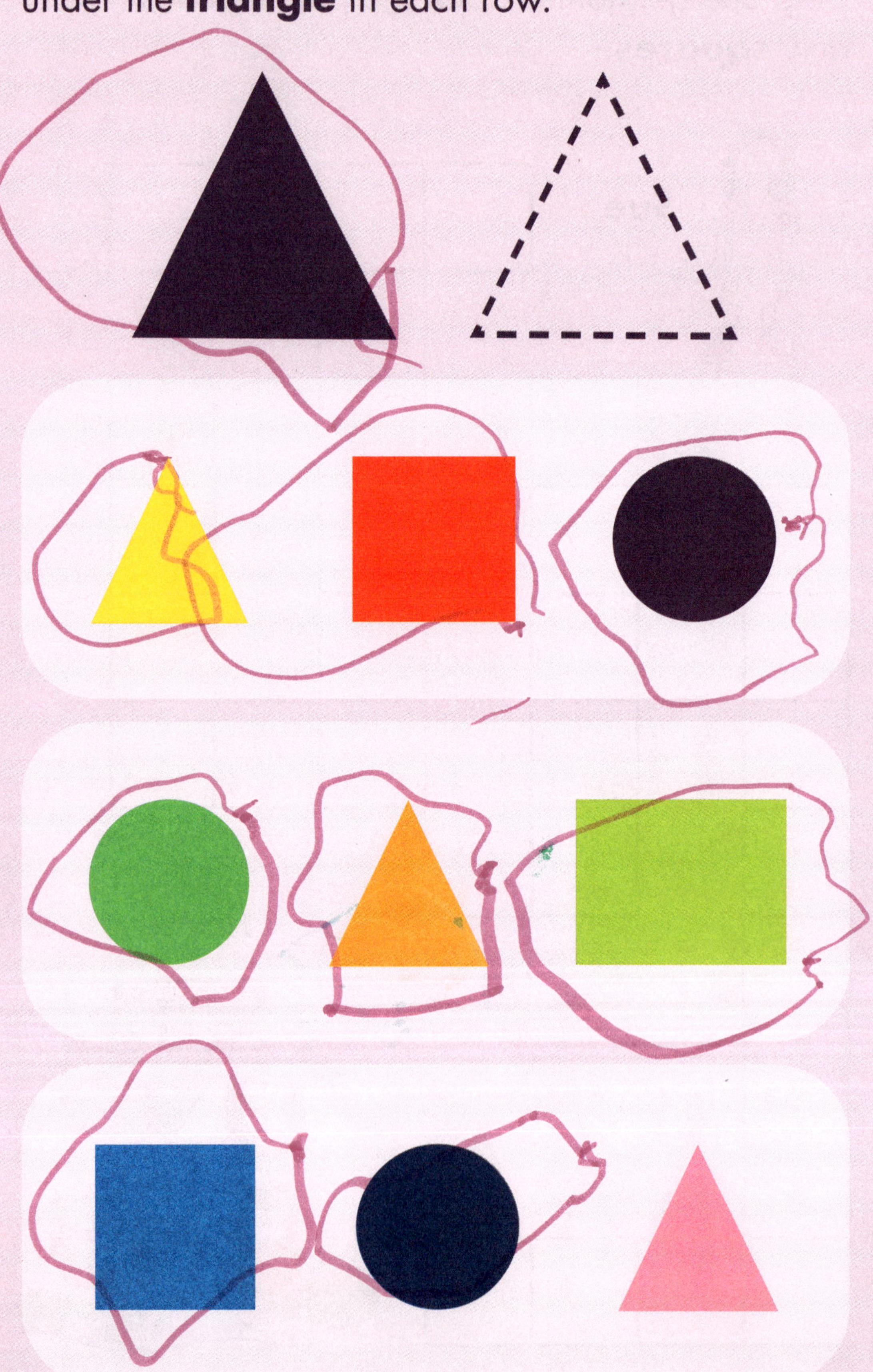

All **triangles** have 3 sides. **Triangles** can be different sizes. Trace and color the **triangle** shapes below.

Rectangles Rule!

Trace the **rectangle** below. Then, draw a line under the **rectangle** in each row.

All **rectangles** have 4 sides, but only the opposite sides are the same length. Draw a circle around each picture that has the shape of a **rectangle**.

Review Shapes

Name the shape at the beginning of each row.
Circle the shape in that row that is the same.

Review Shapes

Color the shapes to complete this picture. Color the **squares** yellow. Color the **triangles** red. Color the **rectangles** green.

Ovals All Over

Trace the **oval** below. Then, draw a line under the **oval** in each row.

Draw an **X** on the pictures that have the shape of an **oval**.

Diamond Days

Trace the **diamond** below. Then, draw a line under the **diamond** in each row.

Help Jim get to the kite shop. Color the path that has only **diamonds**.

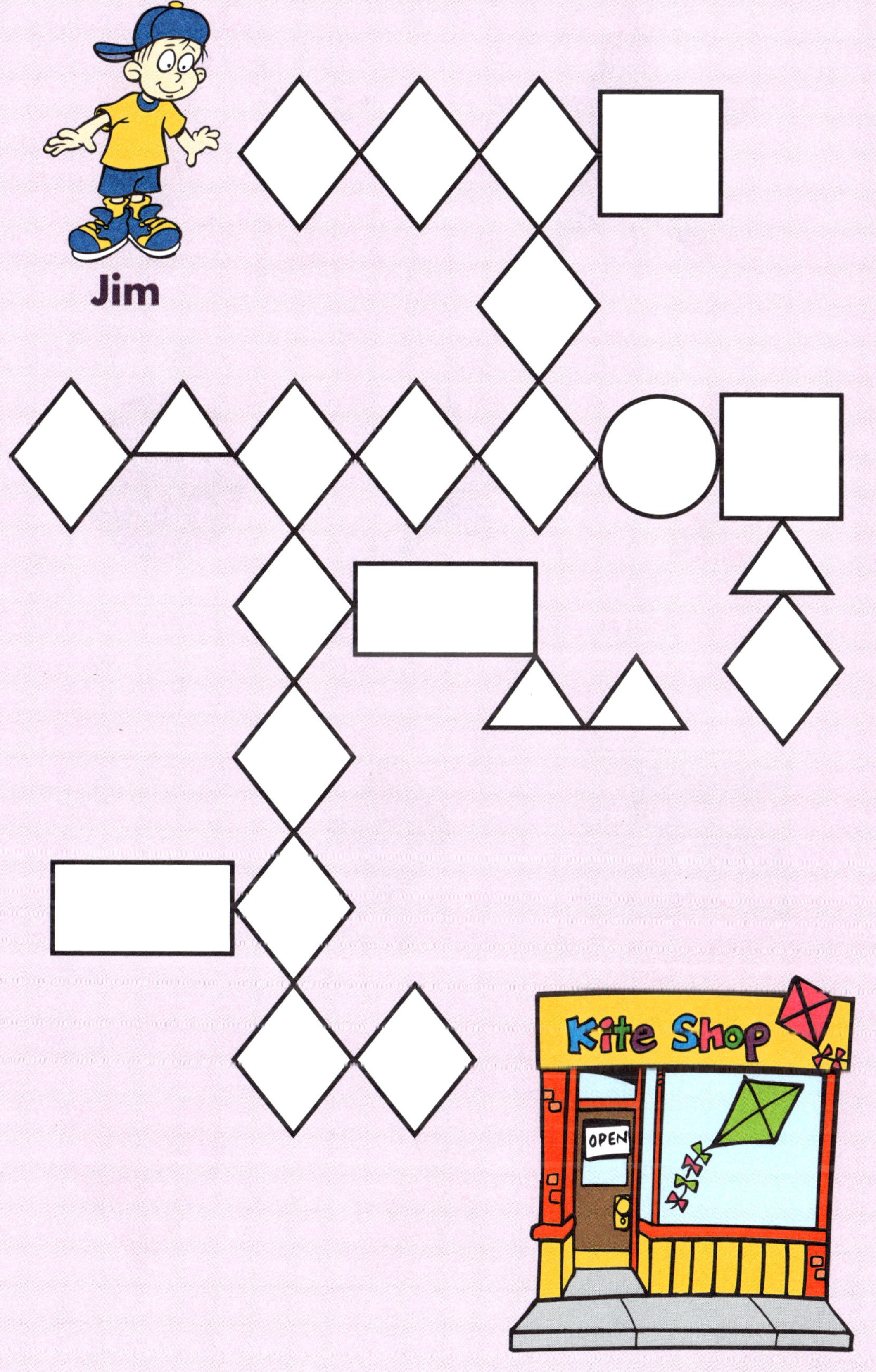

A Star Is Born

Trace the **star** below. Then, draw a line under the **star** in each row.

Connect the dots in order to make your own **stars**.

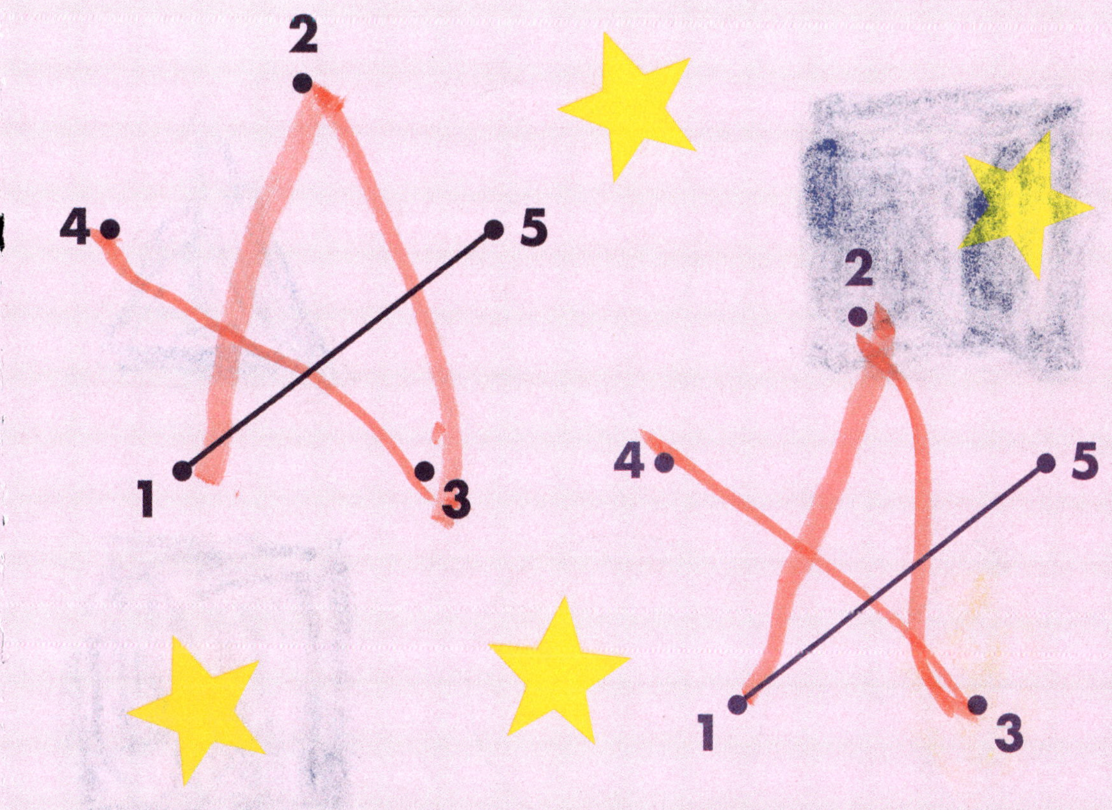

Twinkle, twinkle, little star.
How I wonder what you are.
Up above the world so high,
Like a diamond in the sky.
Twinkle, twinkle, little star.
How I wonder what you are.

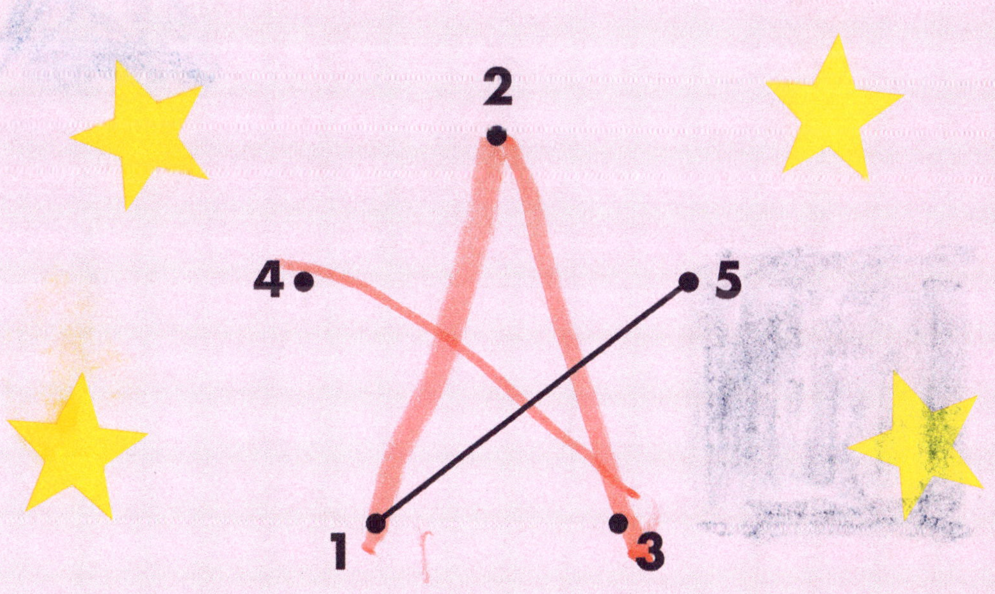

Review Shapes

Color the **squares purple**. Color the **triangles blue**. Color the **diamonds yellow**.

Review Shapes

Trace and color each shape. Draw and color two more of each shape.

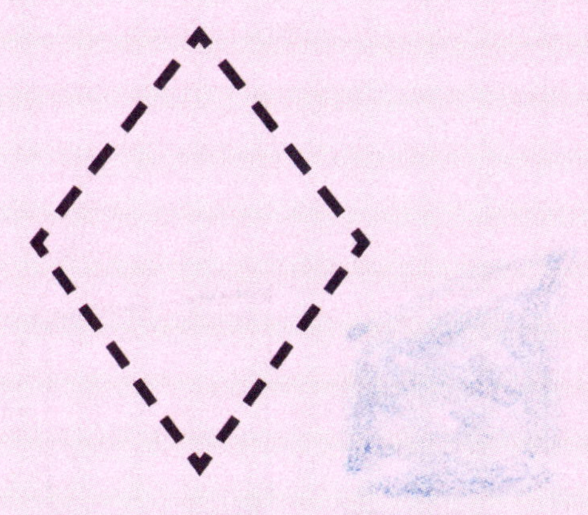

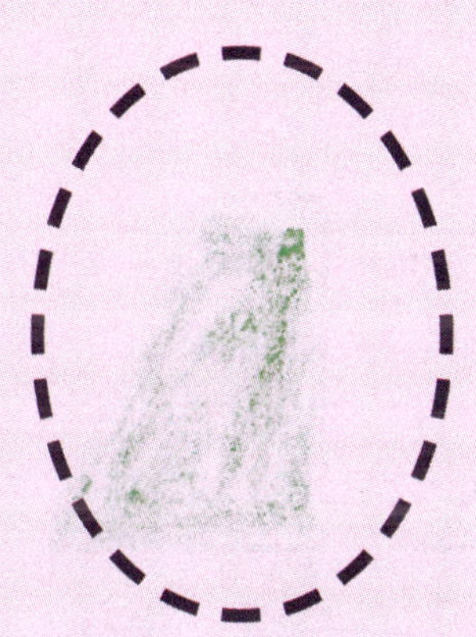

Simply the Same

Color the shape in each row that looks the same as the first shape.

Dare to Be Different

Draw an **X** on the picture in each group that is different.

All Together Now

Color the pictures in each group that go together. Draw an **X** on the one that does not belong.

All Together Now

Draw an **X** on the picture that does not belong.
Draw another thing that does belong.

Opposites Attract

Opposites are things that are different in every way. Draw a line to match the opposites.

day

sad

front

night

happy

back

Opposites Attract

Draw a picture of the opposite.

day **night**

sad **happy**

Measuring Up

Cut out the measuring stick at the bottom of the page. Measure each pencil below.

Example: This pencil is eight boxes long.

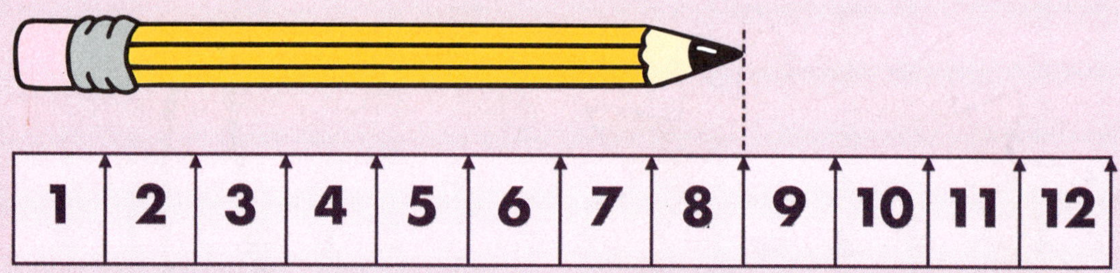

________ boxes long

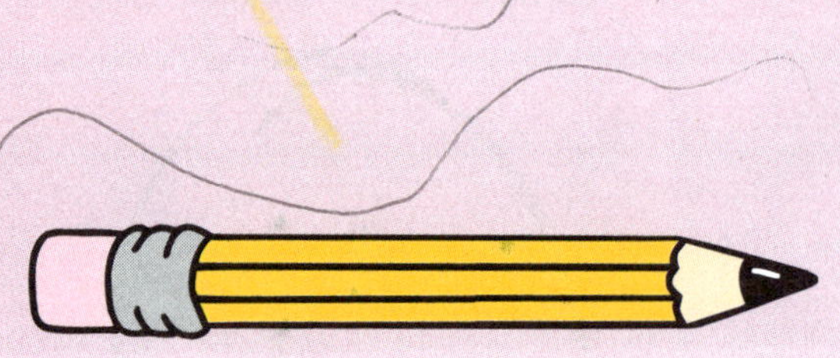

________ boxes long

Draw an **X** on the shorter pencil.
Circle the longer pencil.

1	2	3	4	5	6	7	8	9	10	11	12

Measuring Up

Use the measuring stick from page 40 to measure these pencils.

_______ boxes long

_______ boxes long

_______ boxes long

_______ boxes long

Draw an **X** on the longest pencil.
Circle the shortest pencil.

What's Up?

Color the pictures above the clouds first. Then, color the pictures below the clouds

Writing Readiness

Top to Bottom

Draw a line from the top picture to the bottom picture.

Snacktime!

Draw a line from the picture on the left to the picture on the right.

Leading Letters

Names are special. We use **capital letters** to set them apart from other words. Circle the capital letters in the names below.

Jacob

Jasmine

Erik

Emily

Lisa

Tom

Anya

Diego

Now, write your name. Circle the capital letter.

Home–Work

Write your address. Draw a picture to show where you live.

Give Me a Ring!

Write your phone number. Practice dialing it using the phone below.

281 448 85 76

Color the numbers in your phone number on the phone above.

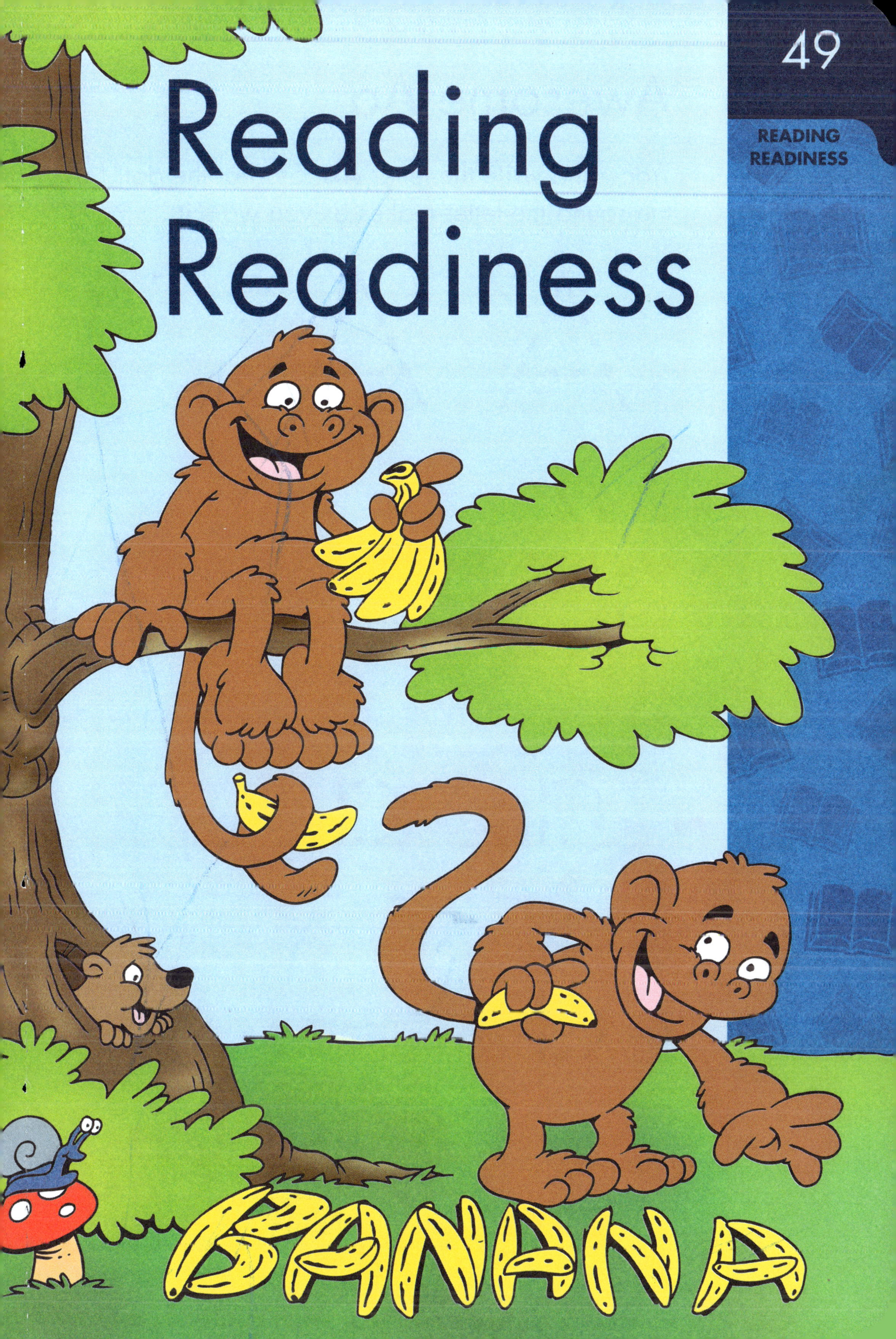
49
READING READINESS
Reading Readiness
BANANA

Awesome Aa

Trace and write the letter **Aa**. Start at the dot. Say the sound the letter makes as you write it.

Beautiful Bb

Trace and write the letter **Bb**. Start at the dot. Say the sound the letter makes as you write it.

Classy Cc

Trace and write the letter **Cc**. Start at the dot. Say the sound the letter makes as you write it.

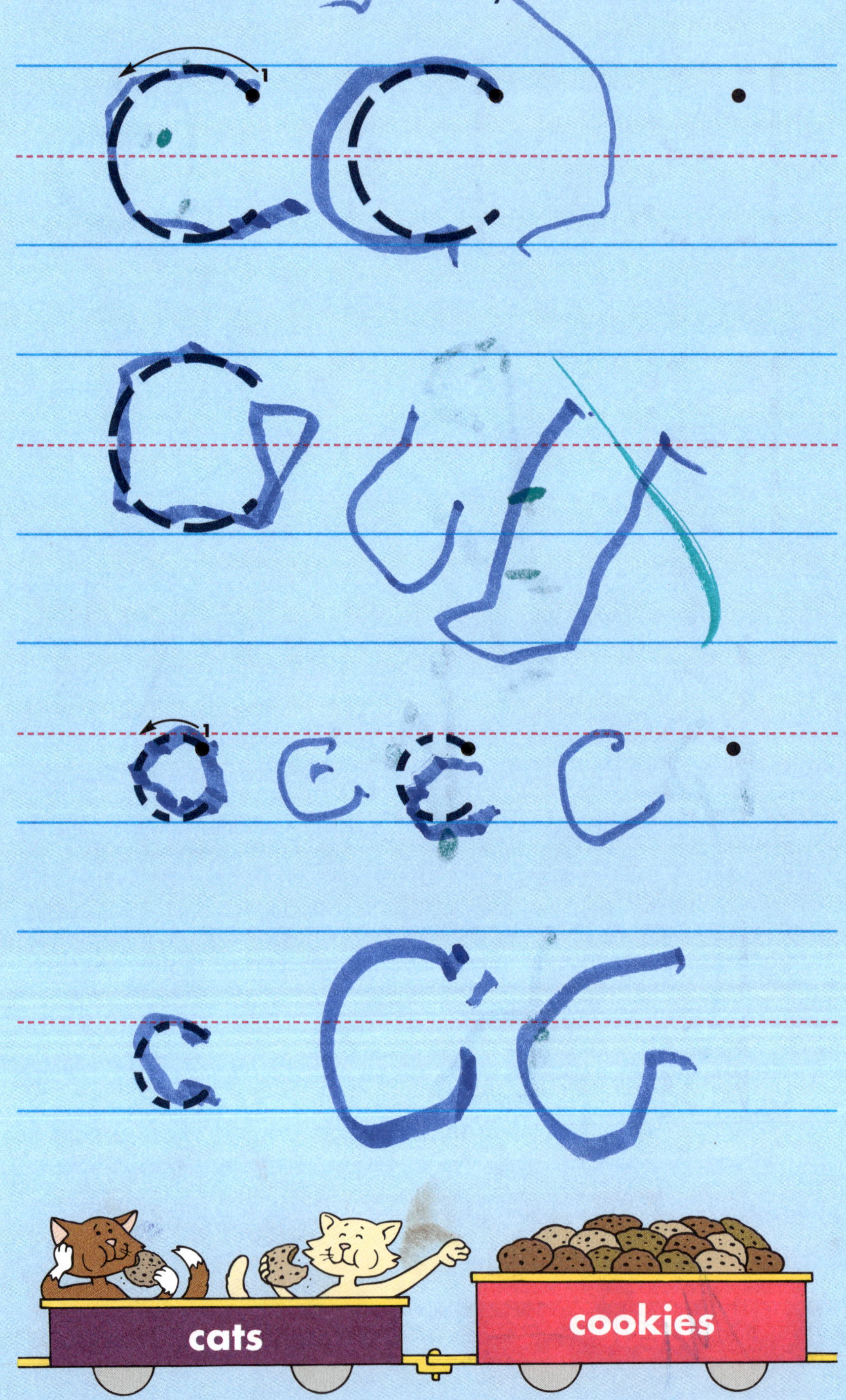

Review Aa, Bb, Cc

Look at the letter each insect is holding. Circle the same letter below.

Daring Dd

Trace and write the letter **Dd**. Start at the dot. Say the sound the letter makes as you write it.

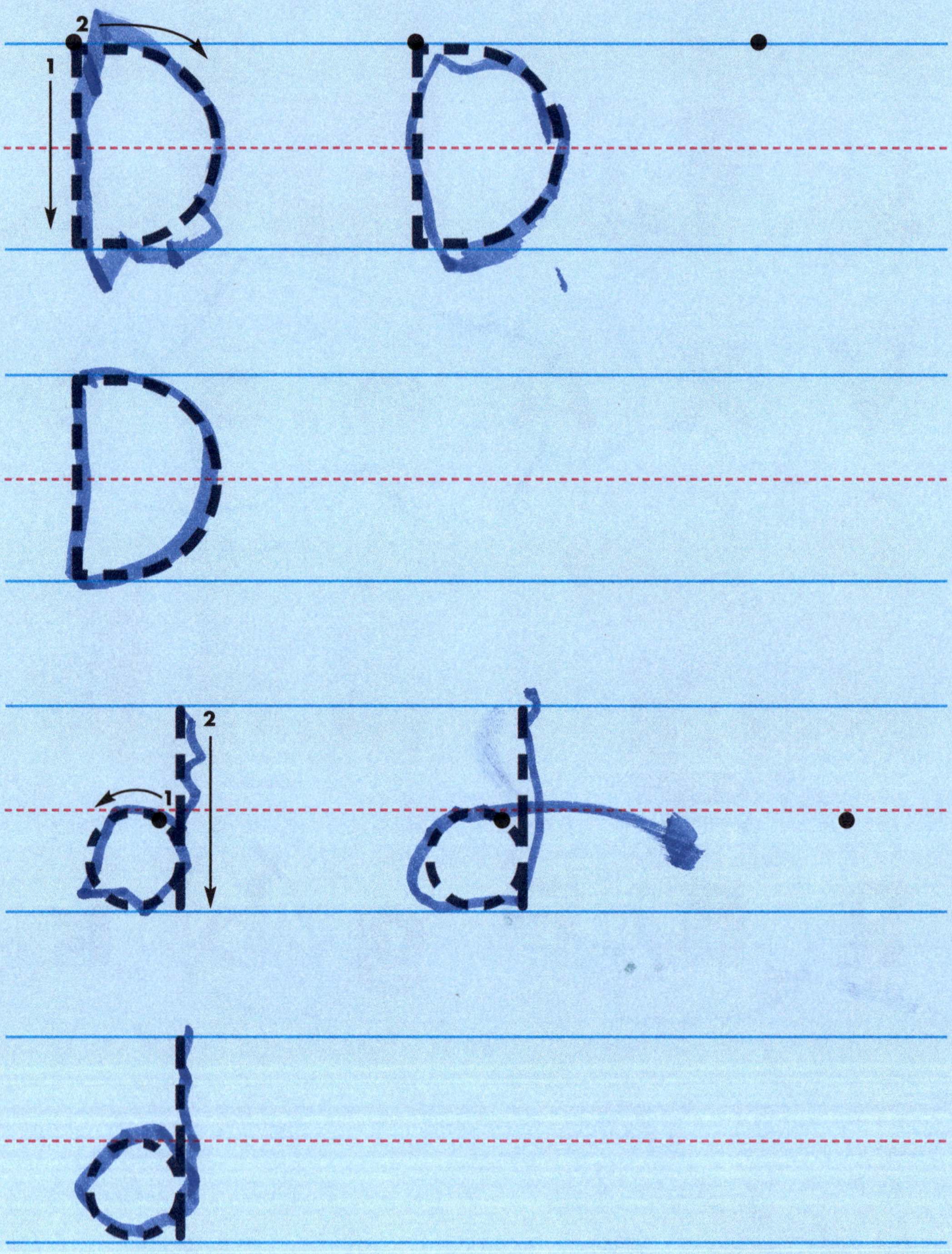

Excellent Ee

Trace and write the letter **Ee**. Start at the dot. Say the sound the letter makes as you write it.

Fantastic Ff

Trace and write the letter **Ff**. Start at the dot. Say the sound the letter makes as you write it.

Review Dd, Ee, Ff

Look at the uppercase letter in each circle. Color each picture with a matching lowercase letter.

Generous Gg

Trace and write the letter **Gg**. Start at the dot. Say the sound the letter makes as you write it.

Honest Hh

Trace and write the letter **Hh**. Start at the dot. Say the sound the letter makes as you write it.

Interesting Ii

Trace and write the letter **Ii**. Start at the dot. Say the sound the letter makes as you write it.

Review Gg, Hh, Ii

Draw a line from each uppercase letter to its matching lowercase letter.

Joyful Jj

Trace and write the letter **Jj**. Start at the dot. Say the sound the letter makes as you write it.

Review A–J

Help the walrus get back to the sea by following the letters in ABC order.

Kindly Kk

Trace and write the letter **Kk**. Start at the dot. Say the sound the letter makes as you write it.

Lovely Ll

Trace and write the letter **Ll**. Start at the dot. Say the sound the letter makes as you write it.

Review Jj, Kk, Ll

Draw a line from each uppercase letter to its matching lowercase letter. Then, color the pictures.

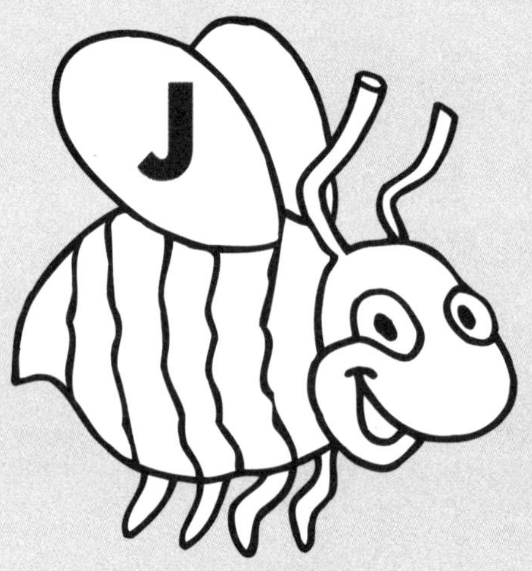

Mighty Mm

Trace and write the letter **Mm**. Start at the dot. Say the sound the letter makes as you write it.

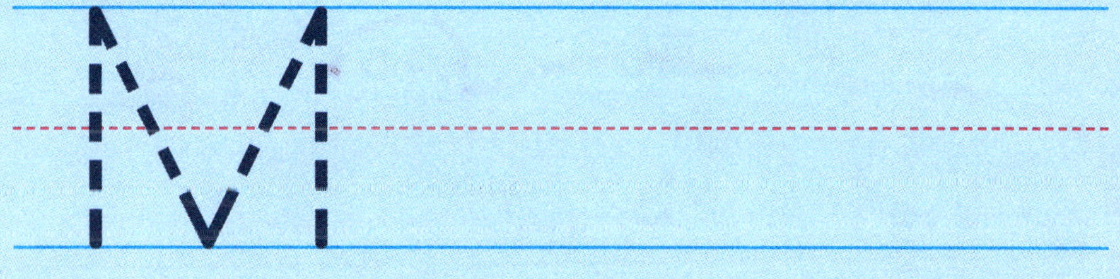

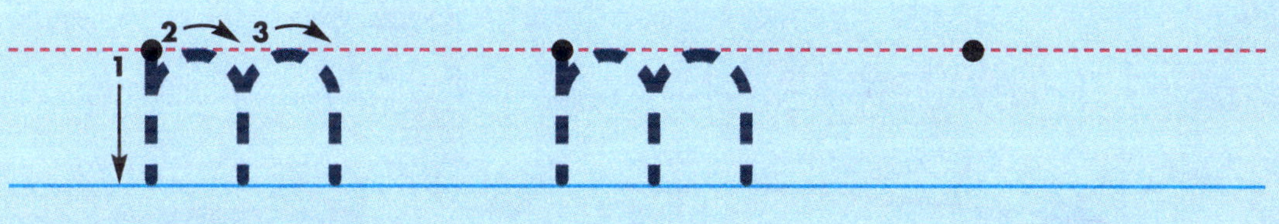

Review Aa–Mm

Help Adam get to the playground. Follow the letters in ABC order.

Nifty Nn

Trace and write the letter **Nn**. Start at the dot. Say the sound the letter makes as you write it.

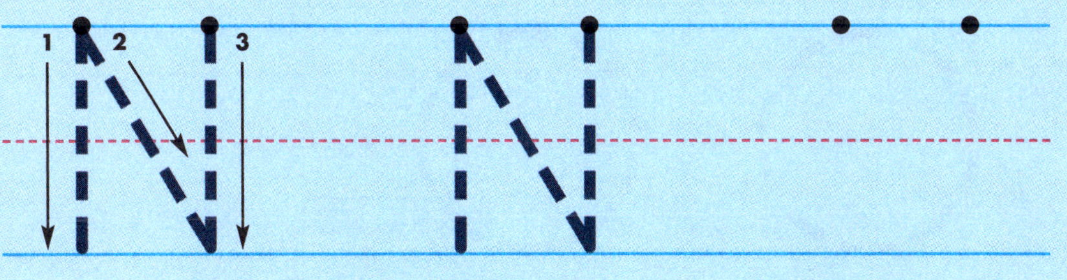

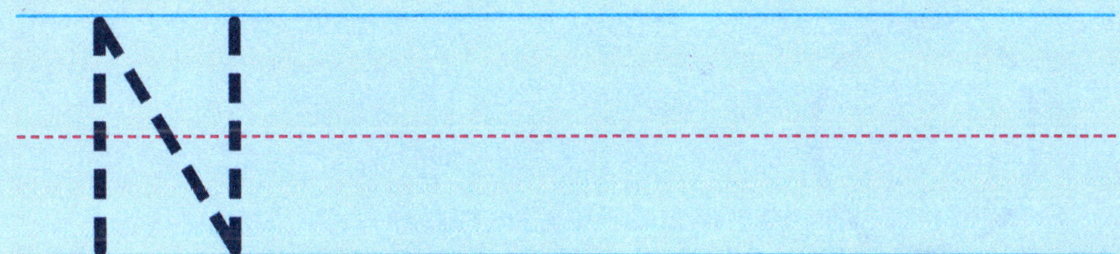

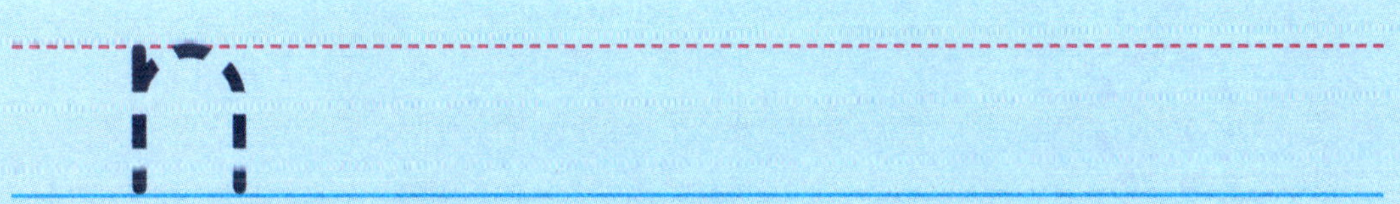

Ordinary Oo

Trace and write the letter **Oo**. Start at the dot. Say the sound the letter makes as you write it.

Review Mm, Nn, Oo

Color each fish that has an uppercase and lowercase letter that match.

Popular Pp

Trace and write the letter **Pp**. Start at the dot. Say the sound the letter makes as you write it.

Quiet Qq

Trace and write the letter **Qq**. Start at the dot. Say the sound the letter makes as you write it.

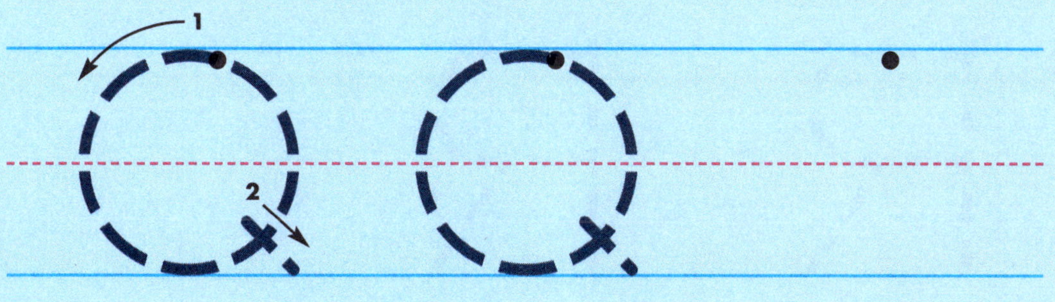

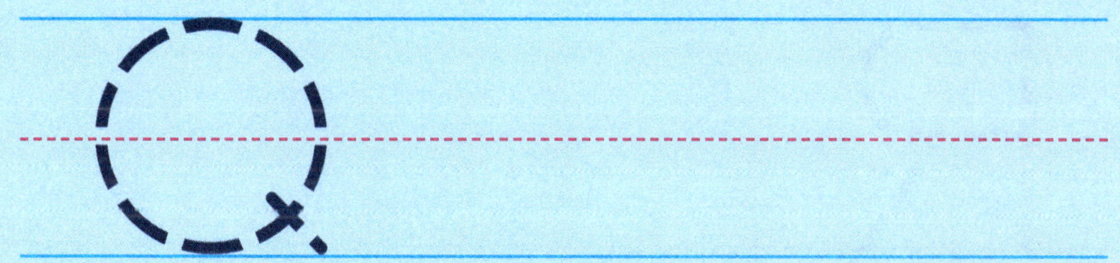

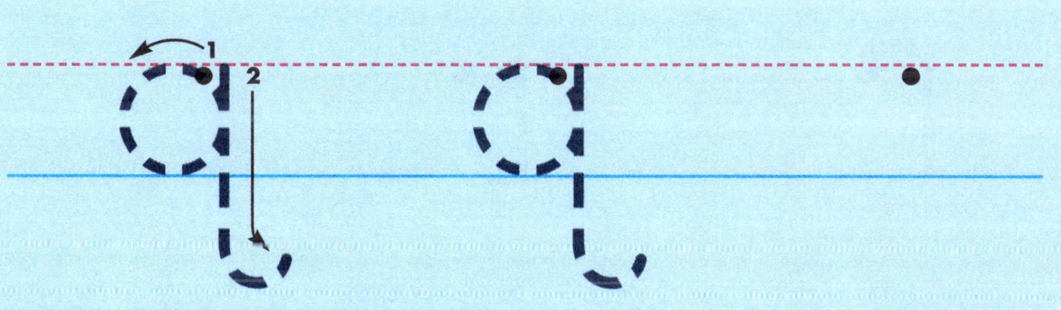

Remarkable Rr

Trace and write the letter **Rr**. Start at the dot. Say the sound the letter makes as you write it.

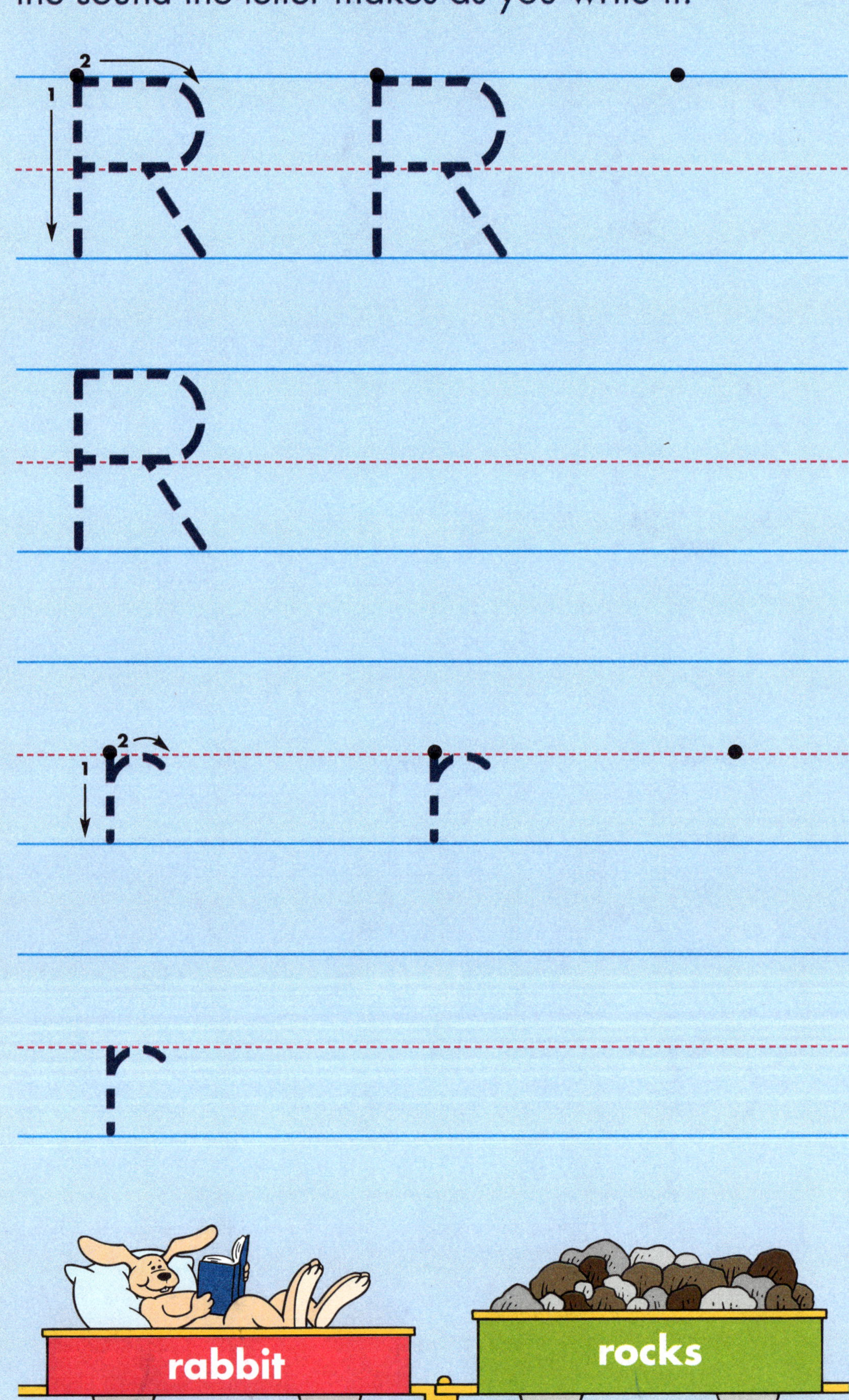

Super Ss

Trace and write the letter **Ss**. Start at the dot. Say the sound the letter makes as you write it.

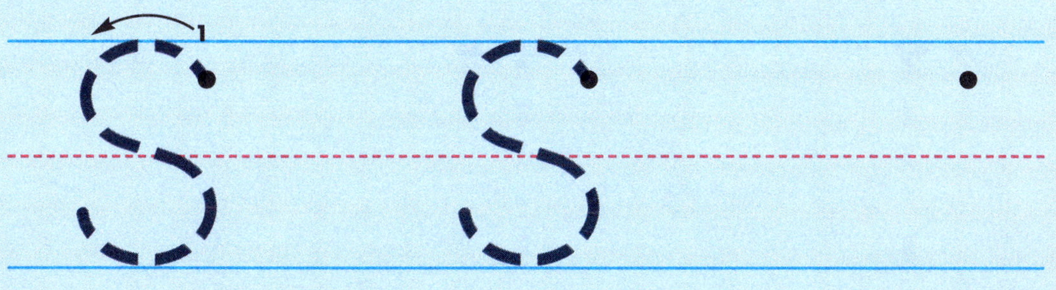

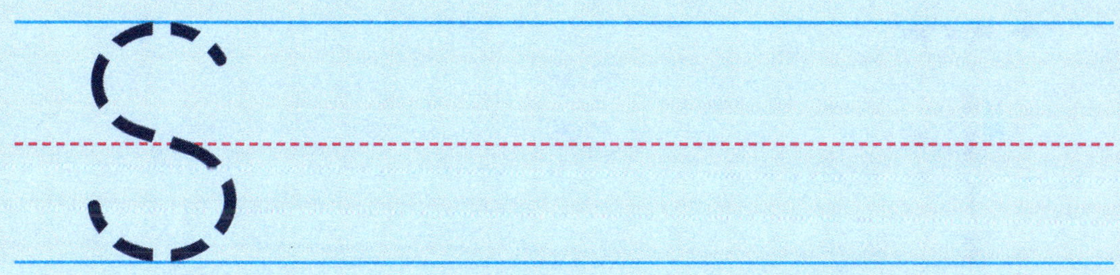

Terrific Tt

Trace and write the letter **Tt**. Start at the dot. Say the sound the letter makes as you write it.

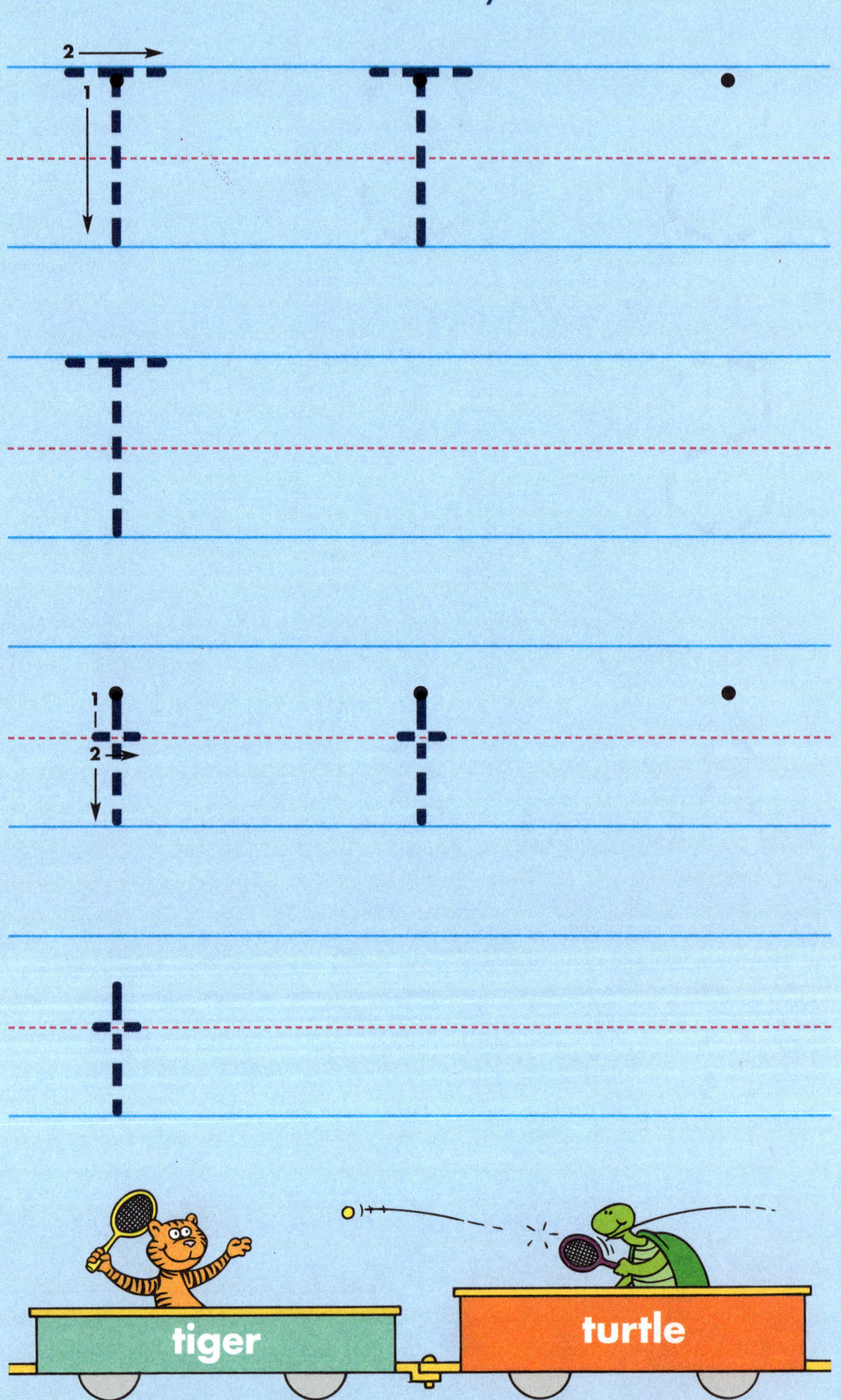

Review Pp–Tt

Draw a line from each uppercase letter to its matching lowercase letter.

Unbelievable Uu

Trace and write the letter **Uu**. Start at the dot. Say the sound the letter makes as you write it.

Valuable Vv

Trace and write the letter **Vv**. Start at the dot. Say the sound the letter makes as you write it.

Wonderful Ww

Trace and write the letter **Ww**. Start at the dot. Say the sound the letter makes as you write it.

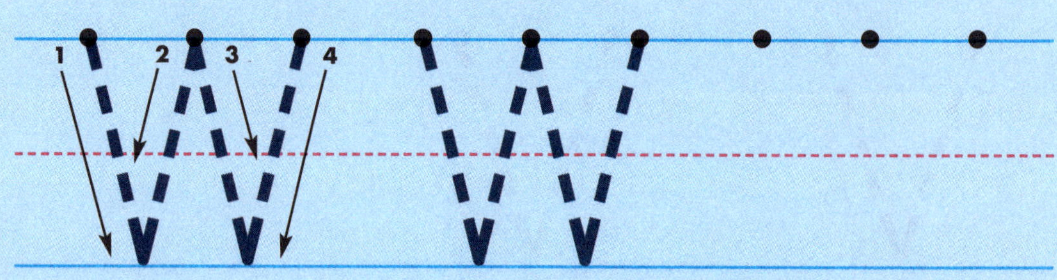

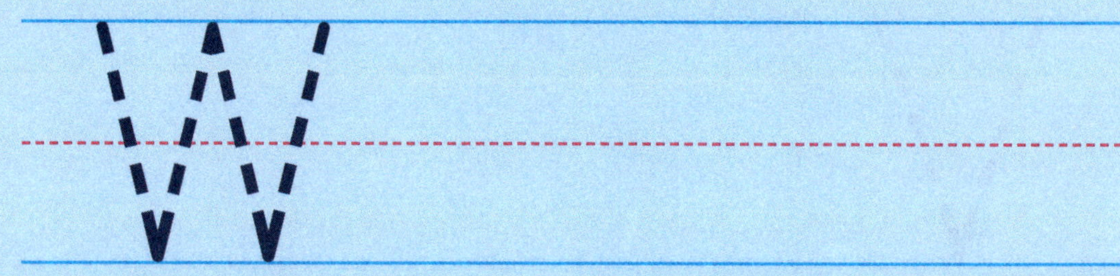

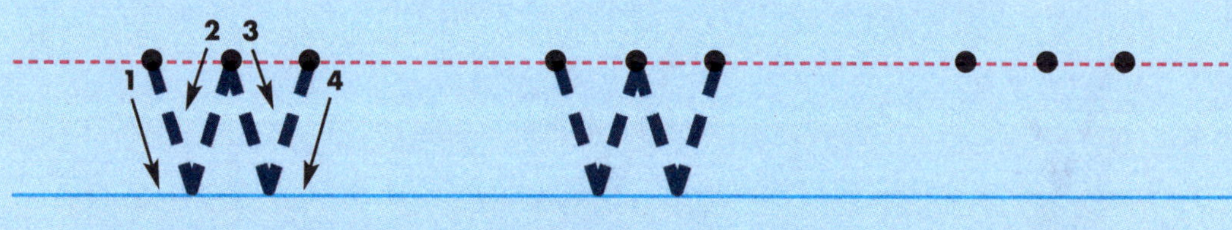

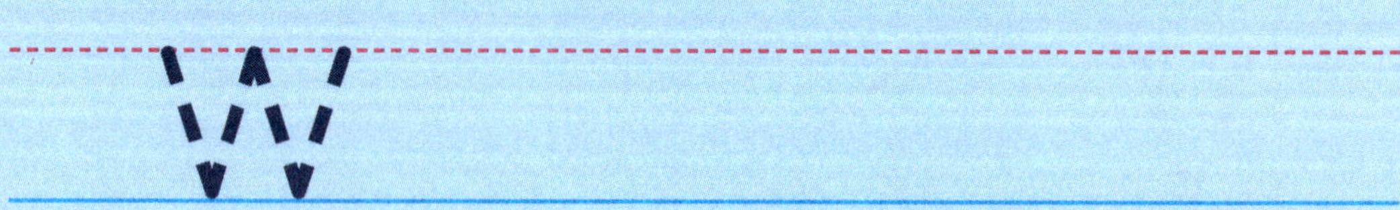

Exciting Xx

Trace and write the letter **Xx**. Start at the dot. Say the sound the letter makes as you write it.

Yummy Yy

Trace and write the letter **Yy**. Start at the dot. Say the sound the letter makes as you write it.

Zippy Zz

Trace and write the letter **Zz**. Start at the dot. Say the sound the letter makes as you write it.

Review Uu–Zz

Write the missing uppercase or lowercase letter for each tie.

Let's Start with ABC

Connect the dots in ABC order. Color the picture.

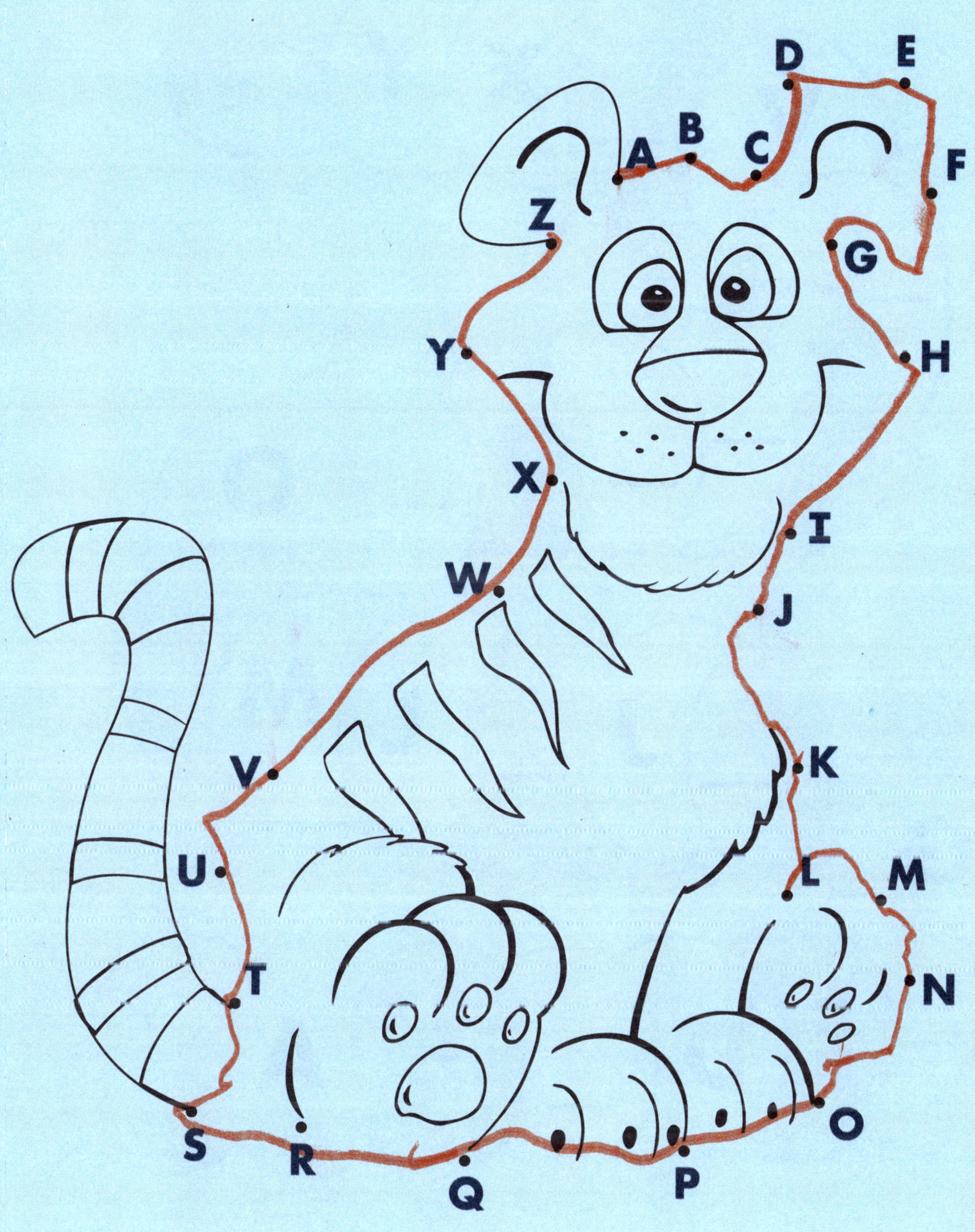

Review Uppercase Letters

Write the missing uppercase letters to complete the alphabet.

Review Lowercase Letters

Write the missing lowercase letters to complete the alphabet.

Sound Off! Short Aa

Short Aa is the sound at the beginning of the word **alligator**. Color the pictures that begin with the **short Aa** sound.

Sound Off! Short Aa

Say each picture name. Write **a** to complete each word below.

Sound Off! Beginning Bb

Say each picture name. If the picture name begins with the same sound as **ball**, color the space.

Sound Off! Beginning Cc

These pictures begin with the letter **Cc**. Color these pictures.

cat

coat

car

Sound Off! Beginning Dd

Say the picture names in each box on the door. Circle the picture whose name begins with the same sound as **dinosaur**.

Beginning Bb, Cc, Dd

Look at each picture. Write the letter for the beginning sound under each picture.

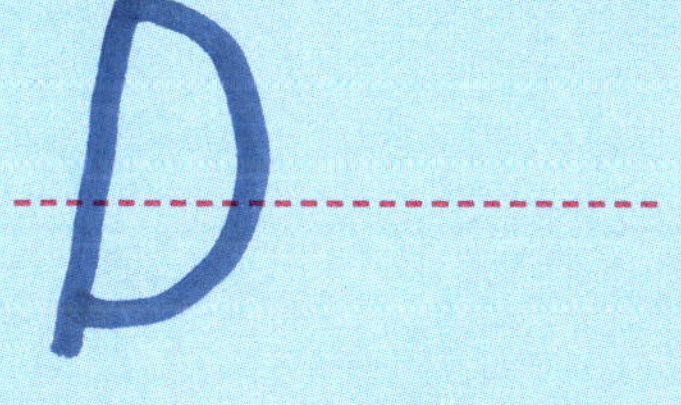

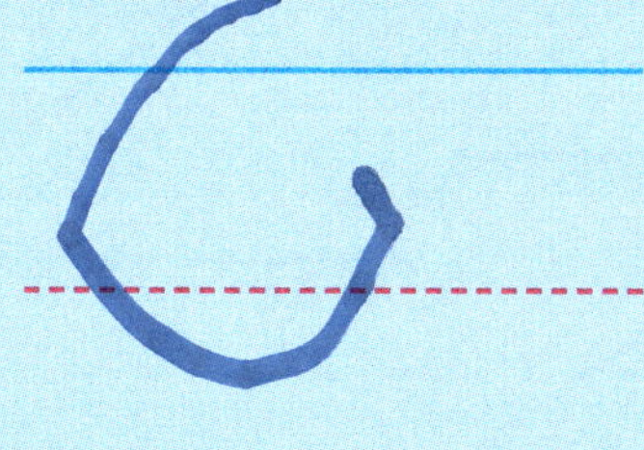

Sound Off! Short Ee

These pictures begin with the letter **Ee**. Color these pictures.

elephant

eggs

envelope

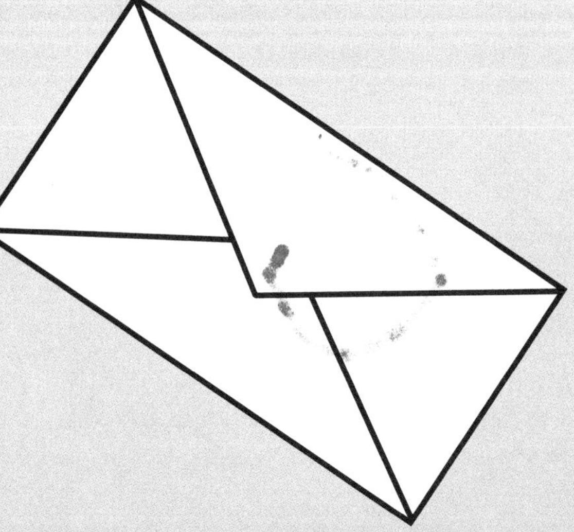

Sound Off! Short Ee

Say the name of each picture. Write the letter **e** to complete each word below.

10

t n b d

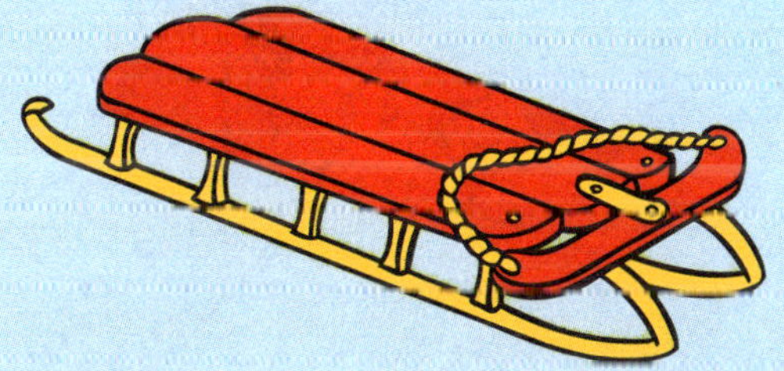

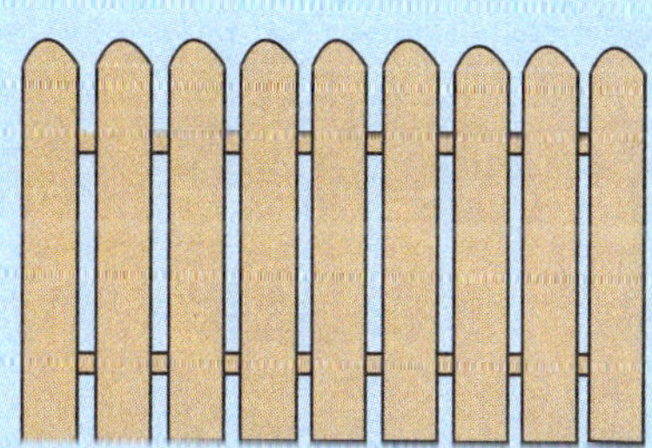

sl d f nce

Sound Off! Beginning Ff

Say each picture name. If the picture name begins with the same sound as **flower**, color the picture.

Sound Off! Beginning Gg

These pictures begin with the letter **Gg**. Color these pictures.

goose

girl

goat

Sound Off! Beginning Hh

These pictures begin with the letter **Hh**. Color these pictures.

house

hat

horse

Beginning Ff, Gg, Hh

Say the sound the letters make. Circle the pictures in each row that begin with the letter shown.

Sound Off! Short Ii

Short Ii is the sound at the beginning of the word **igloo**. Color the pictures that begin with the **short Ii** sound.

Sound Off! Short Ii

Short Ii is the sound you hear in the middle of the word **pig**. Say each picture name. Write **i** to complete each word below.

ch ck g ft

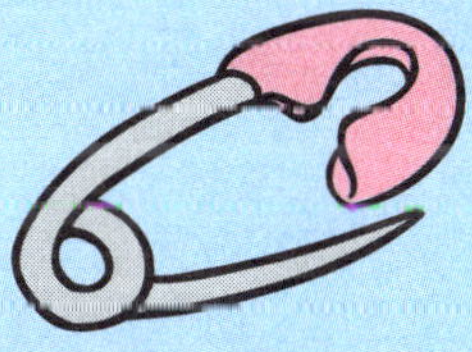

p n w g

Beginning Gg, Hh, Ii

Say the sound the letters make. Circle the pictures in each row that begin with the letter shown.

Sounds Off! Beginning Jj

What is Jamie wearing today? Say each picture name. Color the spaces with the **Jj** sound blue. Color the other spaces yellow.

What is Jamie wearing? ______________________

Sound Off! Beginning Kk

Look at the pictures on the kite's tail. Say each picture name. If the picture begins with the same sound as **kite**, color it **orange**. Then, color the kite.

Sound Off! Beginning Ll

Cut out the stamps at the bottom of the page. Say each picture name. If the picture begins with the same sound as **letter**, glue it on an envelope.

This page is blank for the cutting activity on the opposite side.

Sound Off! Beginning Mm

These pictures begin with the letter **Mm**. Color these pictures.

moon

mitten

moose

Sound Off! Beginning Nn

Help the birds find their nest. Follow the path with the pictures whose names begin with the same sound as **nest**.

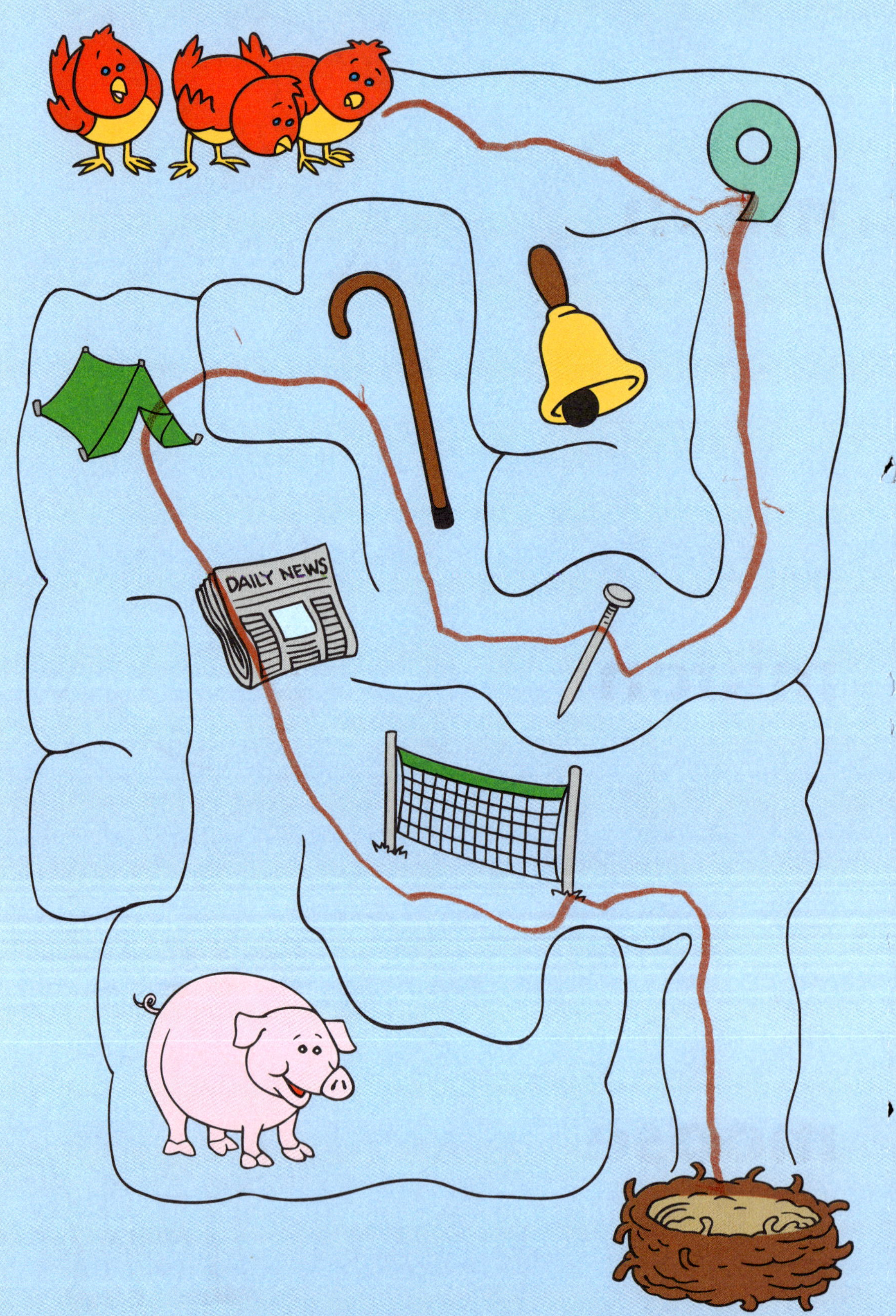

Sound Off! Short Oo

Look at the pictures. Color the pictures that begin with the **short Oo** sound.

Sound Off! Short Oo

Say each picture name. Write **o** to complete each word below.

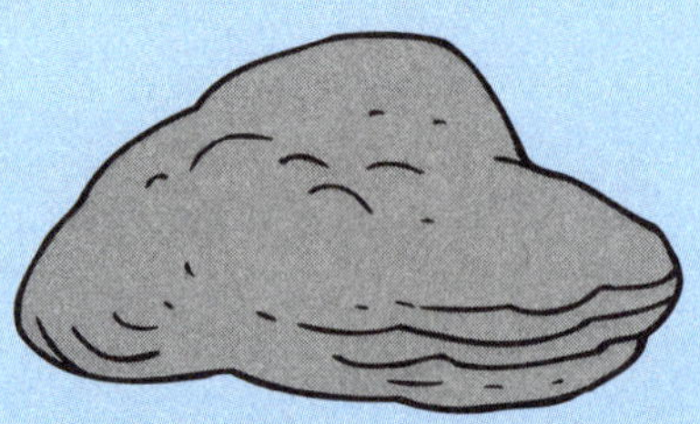

r ck   p t

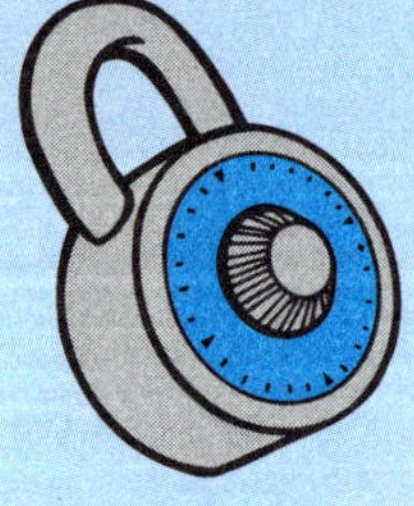

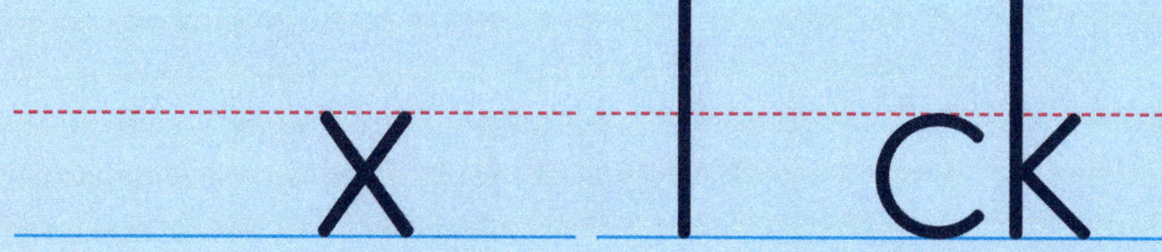

Review Short Vowels

Say each picture name. Cut out the words. Glue each word where it belongs.

hat	pot	hen	fin	mat

This page is blank for the cutting activity on the opposite side.

Beginning Mm, Nn, Oo

Say the sound the letters make. Circle the pictures in each row that begin with the letter shown.

Sound Off! Beginning Pp

Pam only packs things whose names begin with the same sound as **panda**. Say the picture names. Circle each picture whose name begins with the same sound as **Pam** and **panda**.

Sound Off! Beginning Qq

These pictures begin with the letter **Qq**. Color these pictures.

queen

quail

quilt

Sound Off! Beginning Rr

Who is the raccoon going to visit? Say each picture name. Color the pictures whose names begin with the same sound as **raccoon**.

Who is the raccoon going to visit? ______________

Beginning Pp, Qq, Rr

Say the sound the letters make. Circle the pictures in each row that begin with the letter shown.

Pp

Pp

Qq

Qq

Rr

Rr

Beginning Qq, Rr, Ss

Say each picture name. Say the letters. Draw a line from each picture to its matching letter.

Qq

Rr

Ss

Sound Off! Beginning Tt

These pictures begin with the letter **Tt**. Color these pictures.

turtle

tie

table

Sound Off! Short Uu

Short Uu is the sound you hear in the middle of the word **bug**. Help the bug get to the leaf. Follow the path with the pictures whose names have the **short Uu** sound.

Sound Off! Short Uu

Short Uu is the sound you hear in the middle of the word **bus**. Say each picture name. Write **u** to complete each word below.

tr ck

m d

Beginning Ss, Tt, Uu

Say the sound the letters make. Circle the pictures in each row that begin with the letter shown.

Sound Off! Beginning Vv

Cut out the pictures at the bottom of the page. Say each picture name. If the picture begins with the same sound as **van**, glue it on the van.

This page is blank for the cutting activity on the opposite side.

Sound Off! Beginning Ww

These pictures begin with the letter **Ww**. Color these pictures.

wagon

watch

window

Sound Off! Consonant Xx

Write an **x** on the lines to complete each picture name.

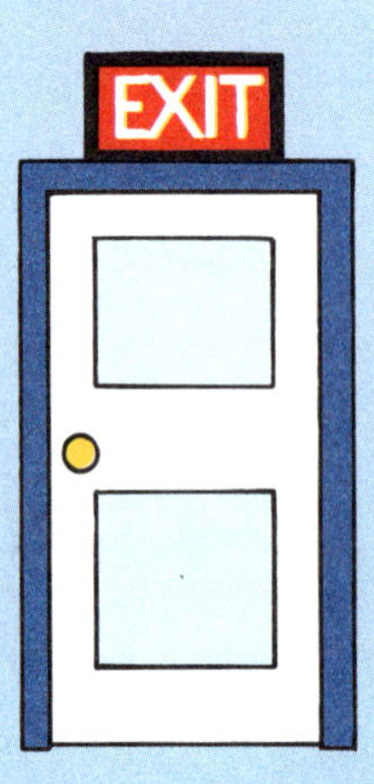

e it

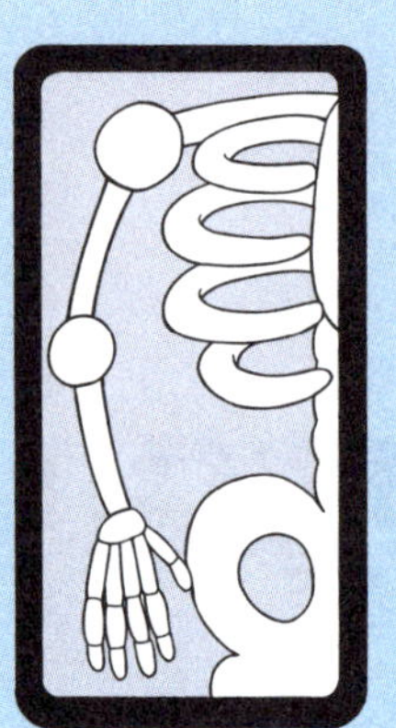

-ray

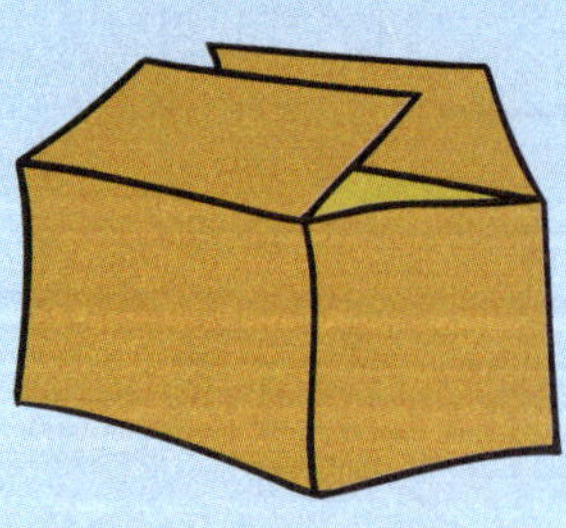

bo

fo

Beginning Vv, Ww, Xx

Say the sound the letters make. Circle the pictures in each row that have the letter shown.

Sound Off! Beginning Yy

Say each picture name. Draw a **green** line from each ball of yarn to the pictures that begin with the **Yy** sound.

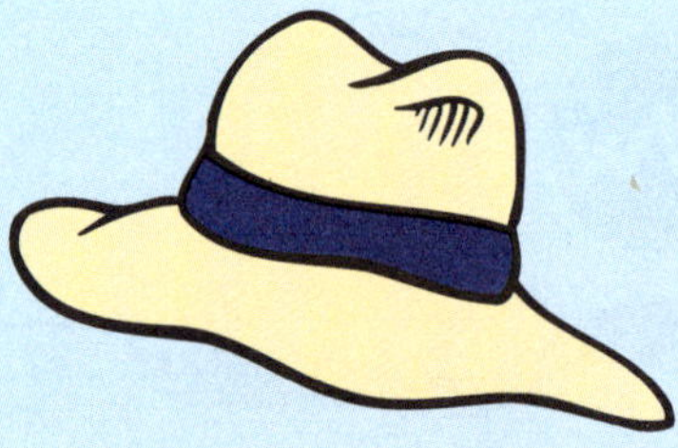

Sound Off! Beginning Zz

These pictures begin with the letter **Zz**. Color these pictures.

zipper

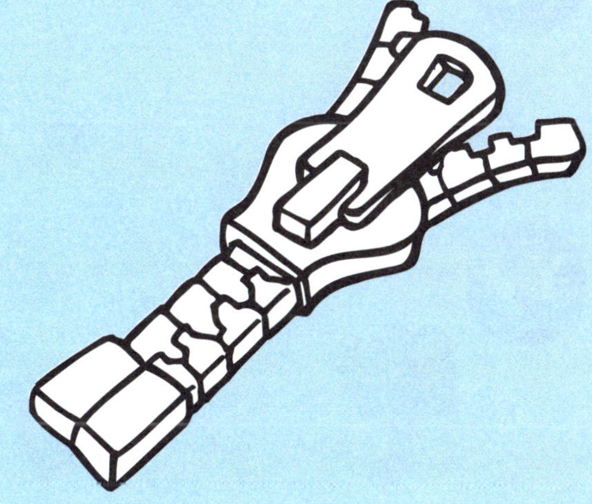

zig zag

zebra

Beginning Yy, Zz

Say the sound the letters make. Circle the pictures in each row that begin with the letter shown.

Yy

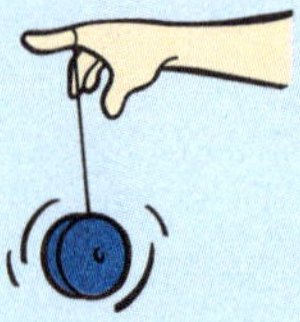

Yy

Zz

Zz

Review Beginning Sounds

Say each picture name. Circle the beginning sound.

t p

n c

b t

b c

t p

c b

Review Beginning Sounds

Look at the letter in each box. Circle the picture that begins with that sound.

Sound Off! Ending Sounds

Look at the picture in each box. Color the pictures in that row that end with the same sound.

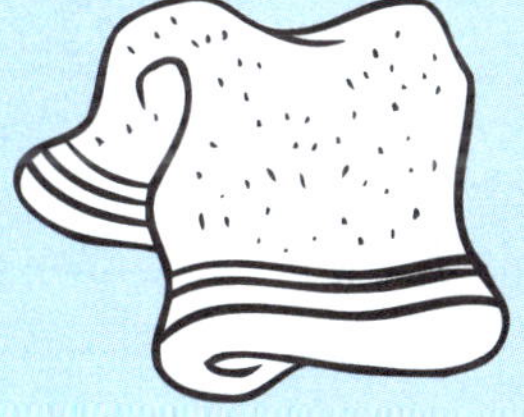

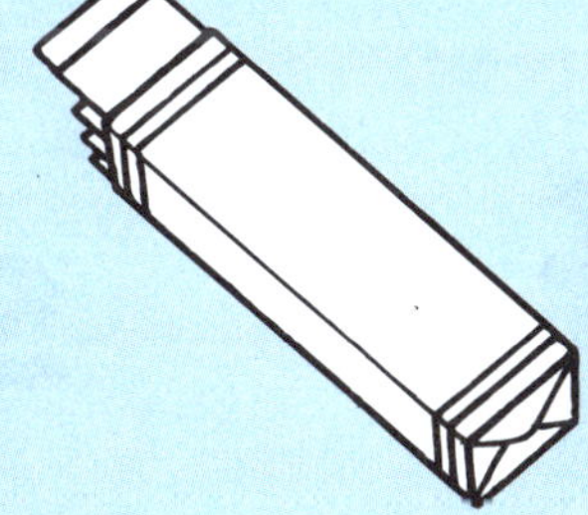

Sound Off! Ending Sounds

Look at the picture in each box. Circle the ending sound for each picture.

d t

b p

x s

n m

g f

s b

Sound Off! Ending Sounds

Say the name of each picture. Write the letter to complete each word.

ja

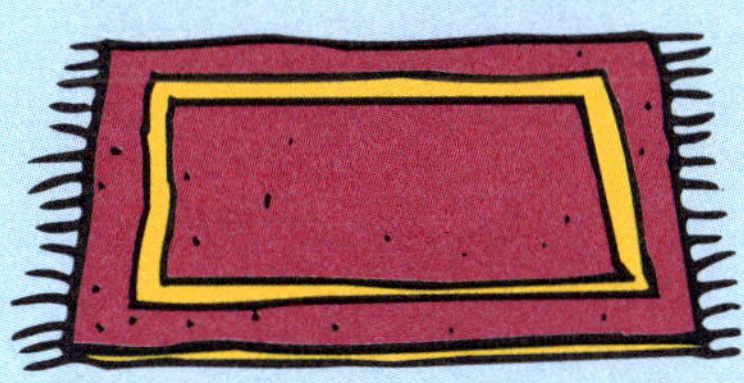

ru

pi

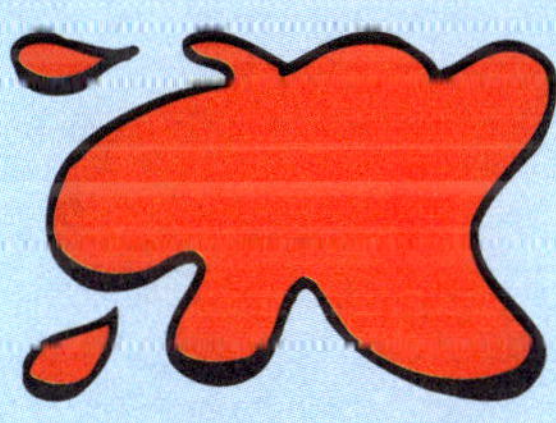

re

Review Short Vowels

Say the name of each picture. Write the letter to complete each word.

c p   p g

d g    p n

b ll 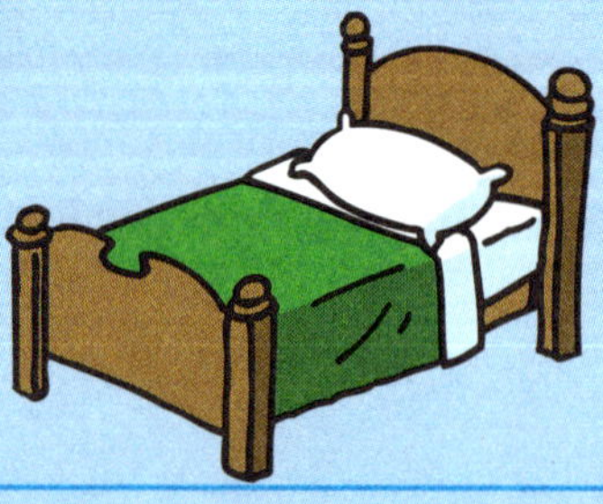   b d

A–Maze–Ing Vowels

Color your way through the maze by only coloring the vowels. Then, write the five vowels below.

Start▼

a	b	m	d	t	g	r
e	m	a	u	o	d	p
o	i	e	k	i	i	e
h	n	c	w	r	n	a
u	o	i	b	o	o	u
a	p	i	e	a	f	k
e	a	c	s	y	l	j

End▼

_____ _____ _____ _____ _____

Rhyme Time

Words that have the same ending sounds are called **rhyming** words. Circle the pairs that rhyme.

map

nest

dog

frog

hat

bat

kite

mop

can

fan

mouse

pig

Rhyme Time

Read the poem. Read the questions. Circle the correct answer.

Jack and Jill went up the hill,
To fetch a pail of water.
Jack fell down and broke his crown,
And Jill came tumbling after.

Who went up the hill?  

What were they going to fetch?  

Who fell down?  

Match It: People

Draw a line to match each word with its picture.

boy

girl

man

woman

Math Readiness

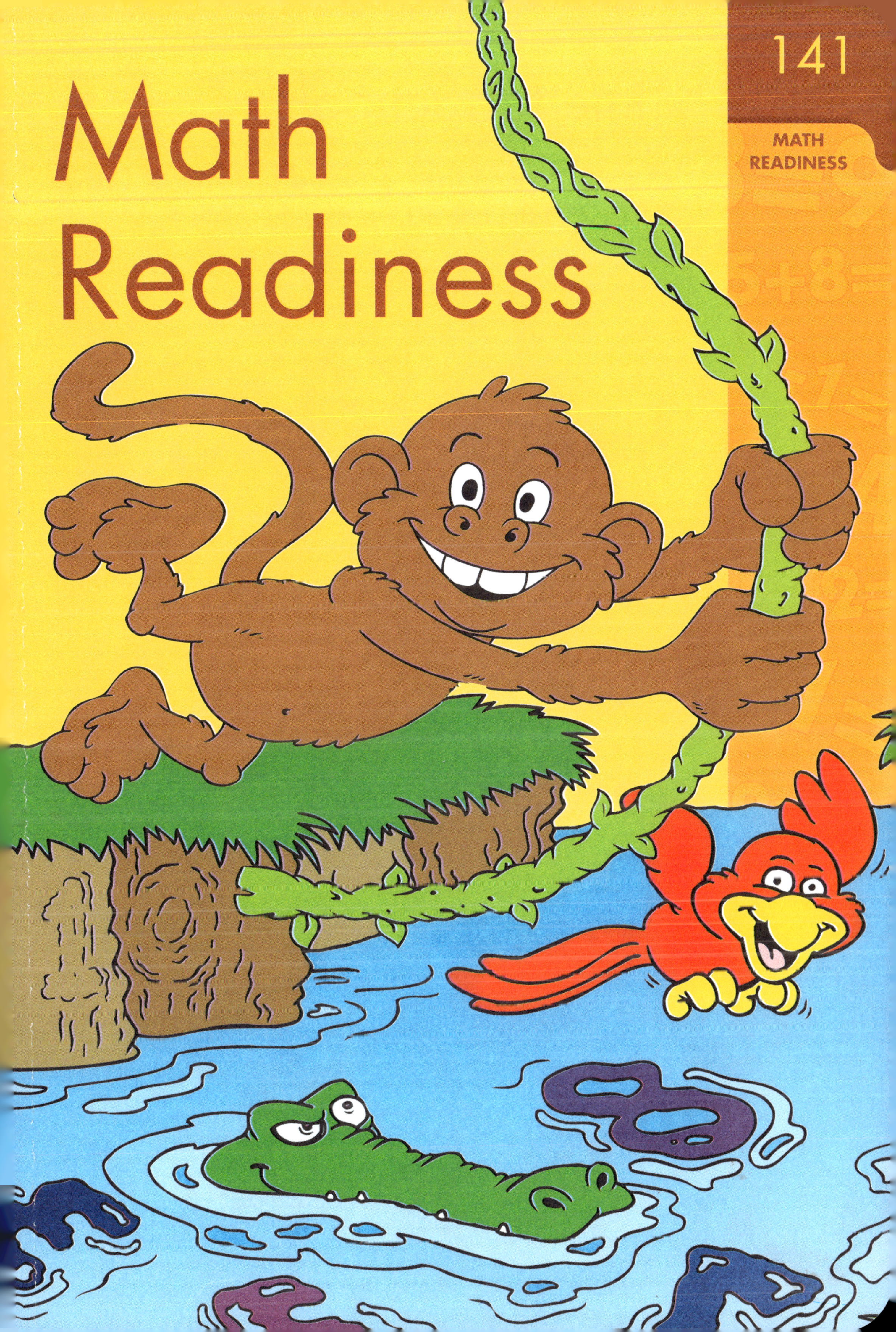

Time for School

What happened **first**, **second** and **third**? Draw a line from the correct word to the picture.

first

second

third

Let It Snow!

Cut out the pictures below. Put them in the correct order. Draw what you think will happen next.

This page is blank for the cutting activity
on the opposite side.

Order Up!

Color the **first** leaf **red**. Circle the **third** leaf.

Color the **fourth** balloon **purple**. Draw a line under the **second** balloon.

Follow the Leader

Circle the **first** thing in each row.

Line Up!

Circle the **last** thing in each row.

More or Less

Circle the group in each box that has **more**.

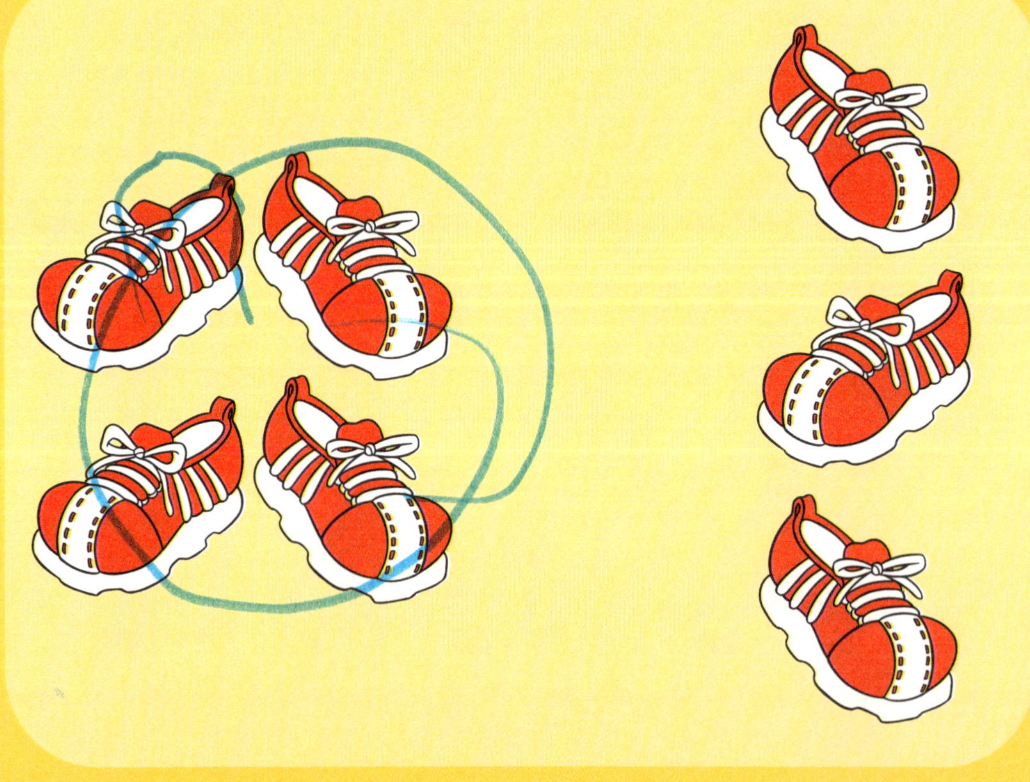

Time for Bed!

Circle the group in each box that has **fewer**.

If the Shoe Fits . . .

One shoe is correct for each person's job. Draw a line to match each person to the correct shoe.

Dog Gone Home

Each dog needs a home. Draw a line to match each dog with a home.

Let's Count! 0

Trace and write the number **0**. Then, draw an **X** on the tanks with **zero** fish.

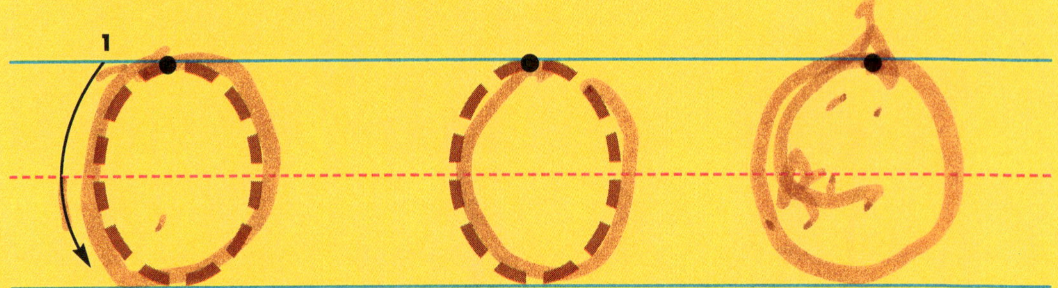

Zero 0

Trace and write the number word. Then, circle the number of fish in each tank.

0 1 3   0 1 2

3 4 5   0 1 2

Let's Count! 1,2

Trace and write the numbers **1** and **2**. Then, count and write the correct number.

One 1

Trace and write the number word. Then, circle each picture that shows **one** fruit.

Two 2

Trace and write the number word. Help the bunny twins catch their balloons. Follow the **twos** through the maze.

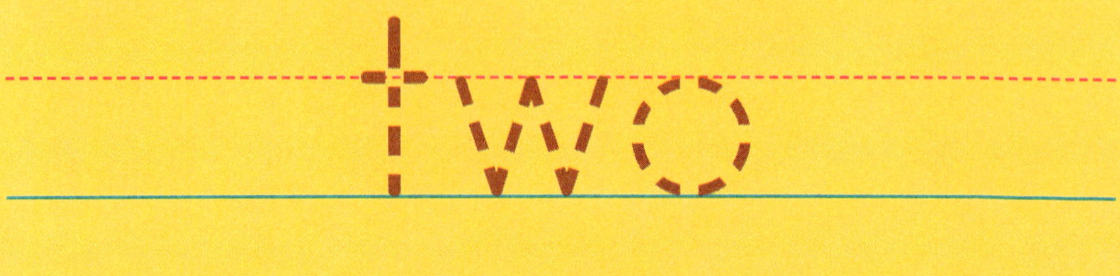

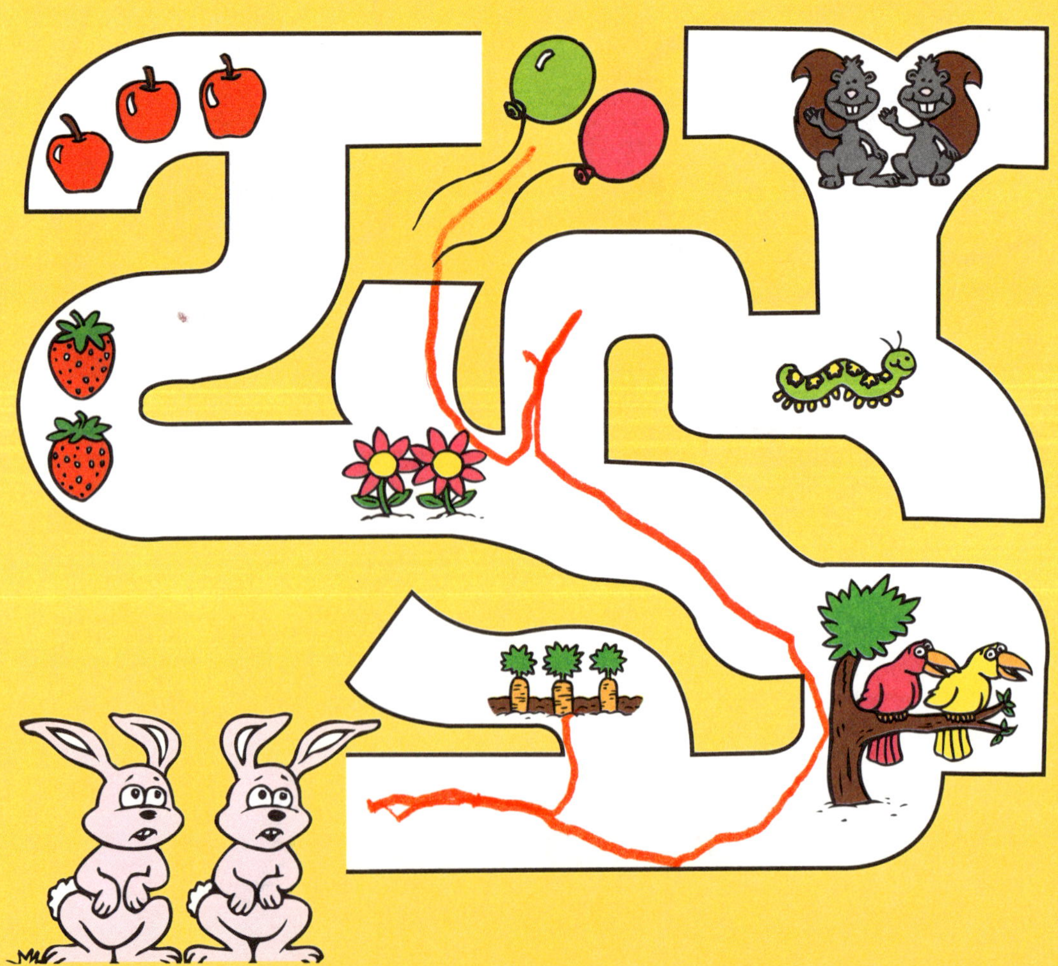

One and Two

Count and write the number in each box. Circle the groups of **one**. Color the groups of **two**.

Let's Count! 3,4

Trace and write the numbers **3** and **4**. Then, count and write the correct number.

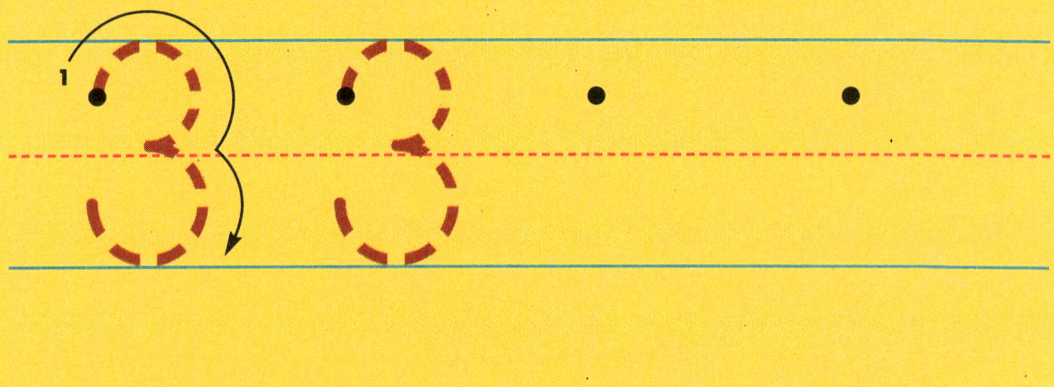

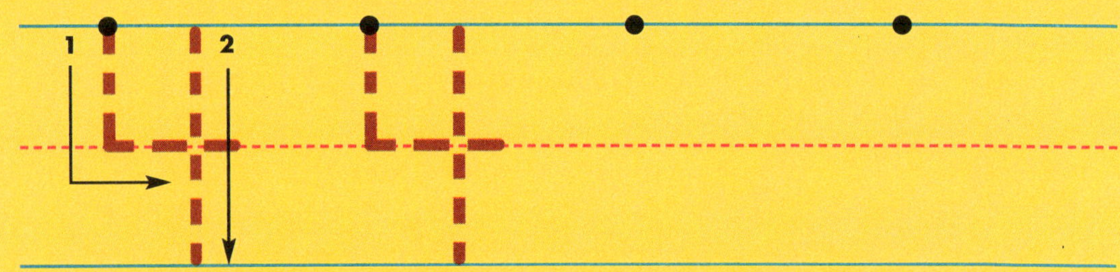

Three 3

Trace and write the number word. Then, write the number of things under each picture.

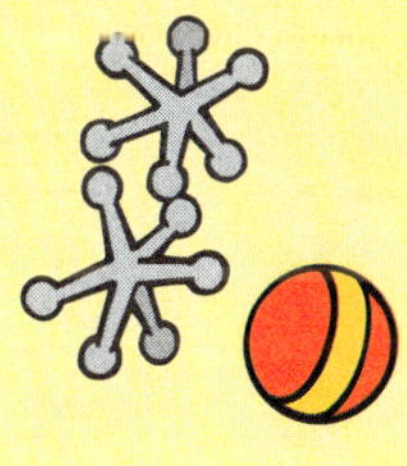

Four 4

Trace and write the number word. Then, complete the picture by drawing **four** fish and **four** seagulls.

Three and Four

Count and write the number in each box. Circle the groups of **three**. Color the groups of **four**.

Let's Count! 5

Trace and write the number **5**. Then, color **five** dogs.

Five 5

Trace and write the number word. Write the correct number on each domino.

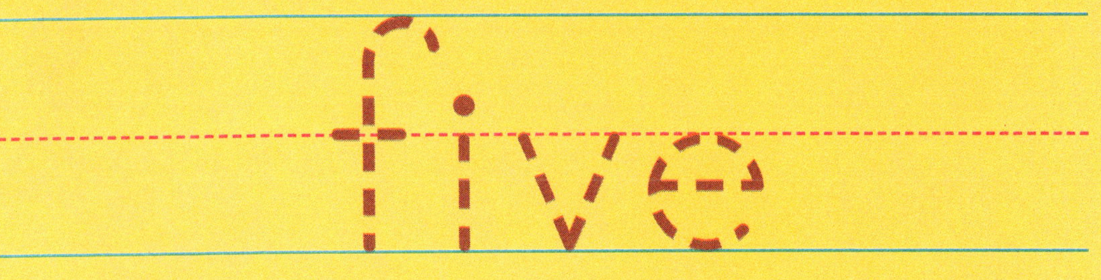

5

Review Numbers 1–5

Look at the picture. Read the questions. Circle the correct number.

How many  in all? **1 2 3**

How many  in all? **1 2 3**

How many  in all? **2 3 4**

Review Numbers 1–5

Look at the picture. Read the questions. Circle the correct number.

How many  in all? **3 4 5**

How many  in all? **3 4 5**

How many  in all? **3 4 5**

Let's Count! 6

Trace and write the number **6**. Then, draw **6** coins in the piggy bank.

Six 6

Trace and write the number word. Draw an **X** on each group of **six** things.

Five and Six

Count and write the number in each box. Circle the groups of **five**. Draw an **X** on the groups of **six**.

Let's Count! 7

Trace and write the number **7**. Then, draw **seven** cookies.

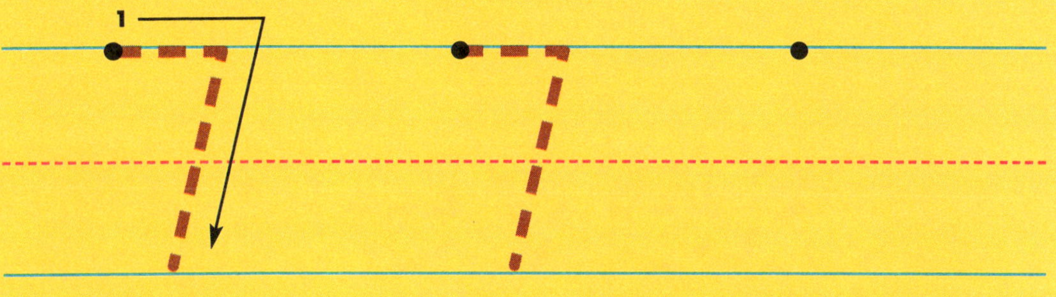

Seven 7

Trace and write the number word. Count the ladybugs. Connect the dots. Color the picture.

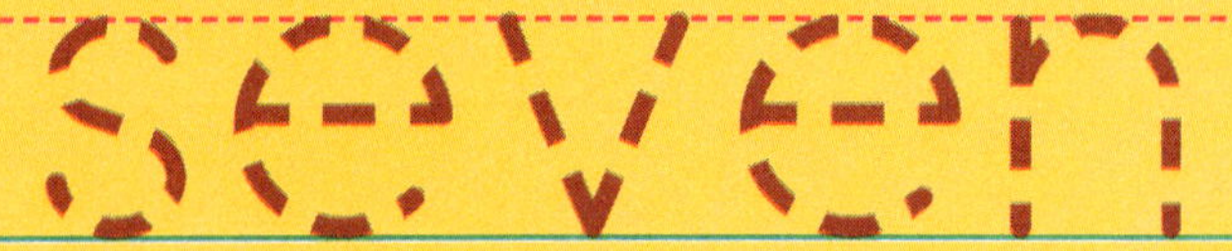

5

Let's Count! 8

Trace and write the number **8**. Then, draw **eight** peas on the plate.

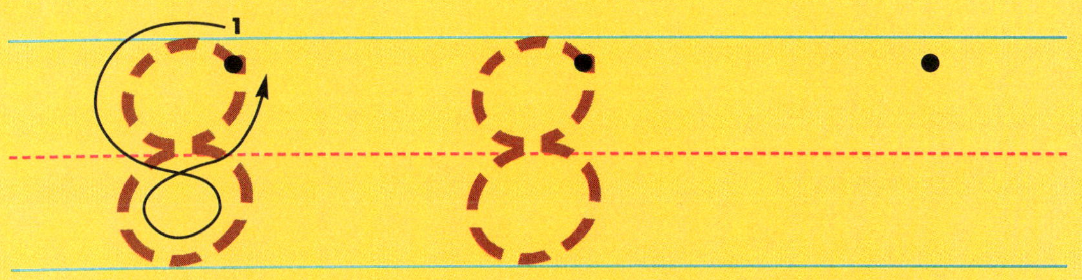

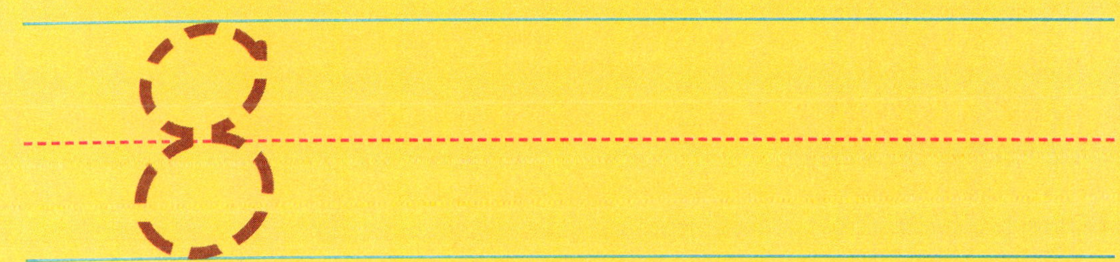

Eight 8

Trace and write the number word. Color the pictures that have **eight** spots.

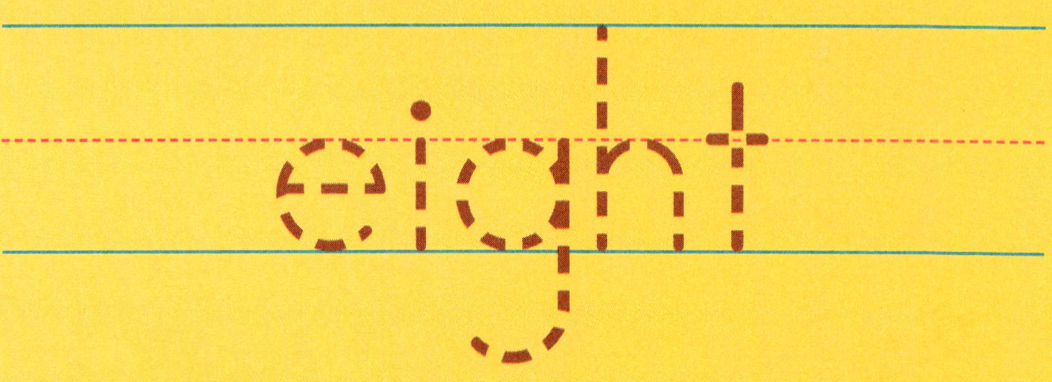

Seven and Eight

Count and write the number in each box. Circle the groups of **seven**. Color the groups of **eight**.

Let's Count! 9, 10

Trace and write the numbers **9** and **10**. Then, count and write the numbers.

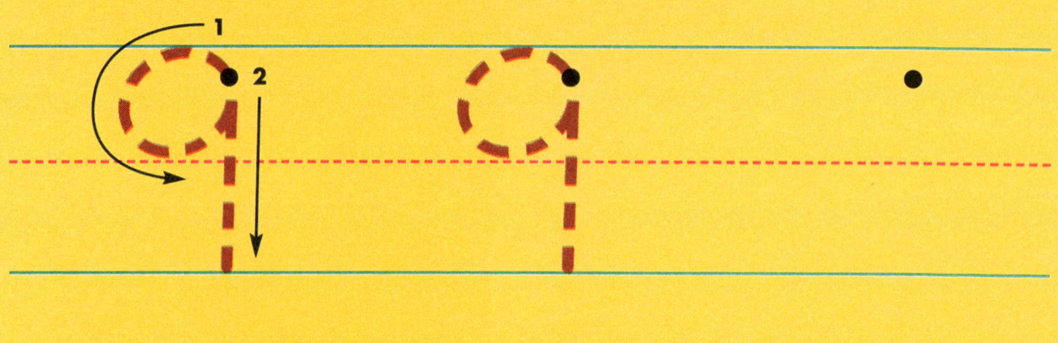

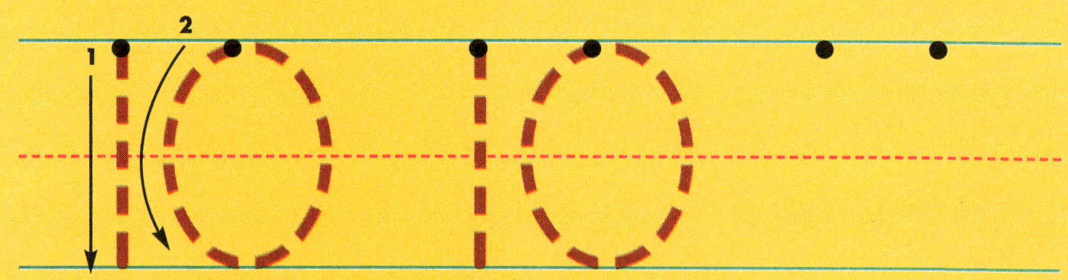

Nine 9

Trace and write the number word. Count the shapes on each quilt square below. Color the squares with **nine** shapes green. Color the other squares yellow.

Ten 10

Trace and write the number word. Write the numbers **1** to **10** on the empty hearts.

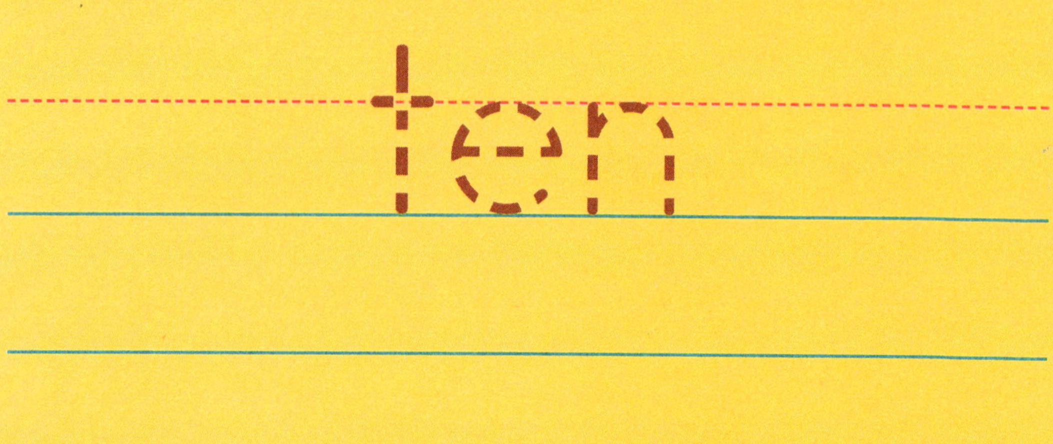

Nine and Ten

Count and write the number in each box. Circle the groups of **nine**. Color the groups of **ten**.

10

10

10 9

Review Numbers 1–10

Count the beads in each group. Write the number.

Review Numbers 1–10

Connect the dots from **1** to **10**. Then, color the picture.

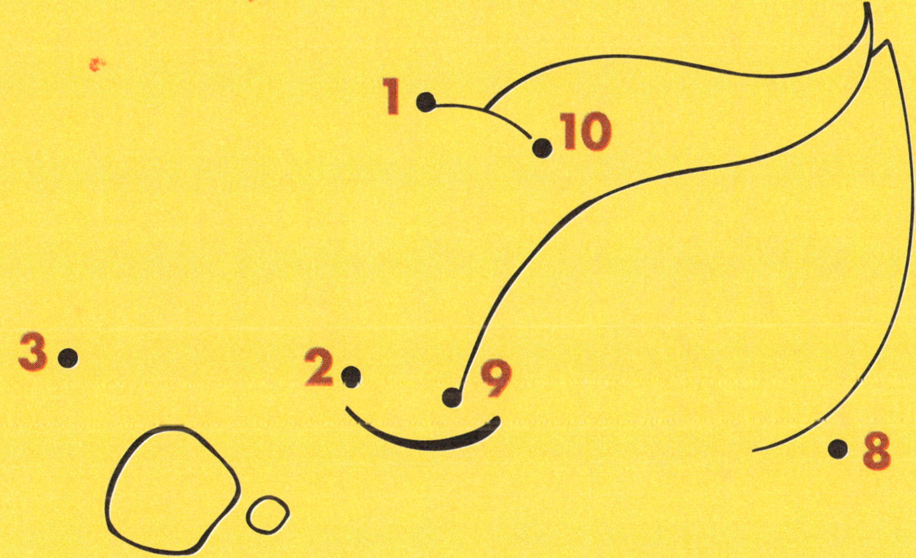

Let's Count! 11, 12

Trace and write the numbers **11** and **12**. Then, count and write the numbers.

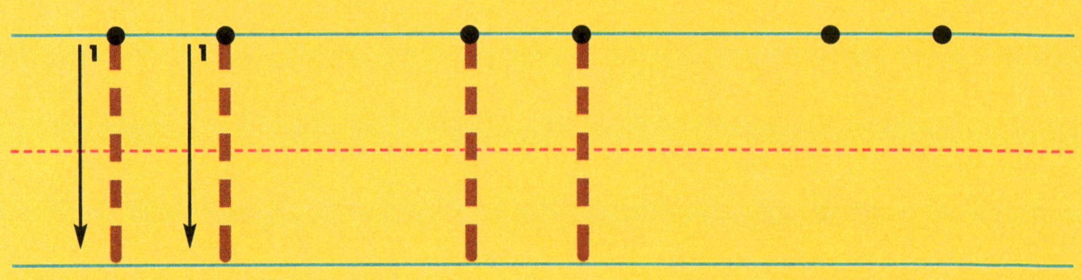

Eleven 11

Count Zeb Zebra's stripes and color them.

Twelve 12

Count each group of creatures. Draw a line from the creatures to their matching apples.

Thirteen 13

Trace and write the number **13**. Complete each puzzle by writing or drawing the missing number of flowers.

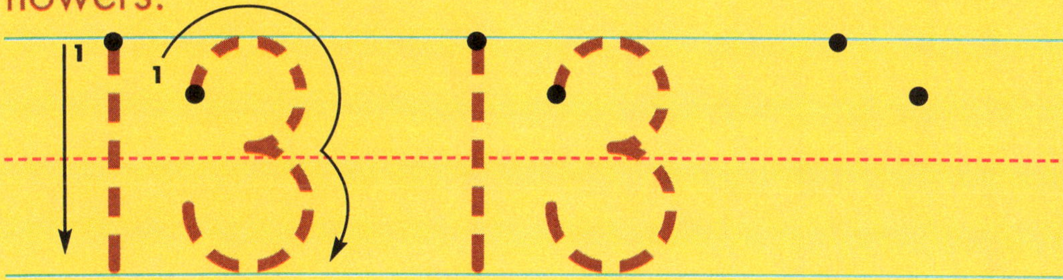

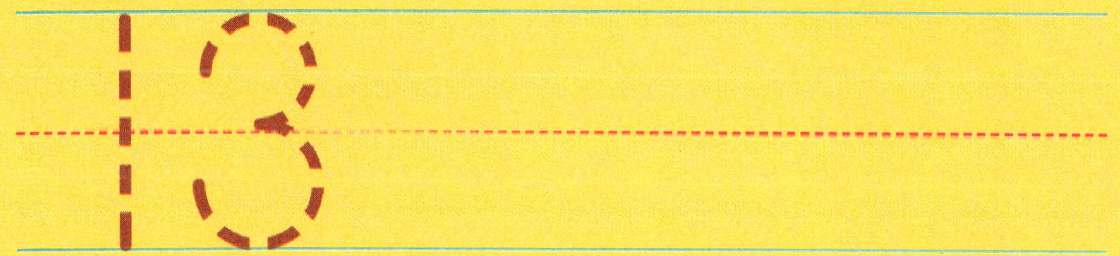

13

Fourteen 14

Trace and write the number **14**. Connect the dots. Color the picture.

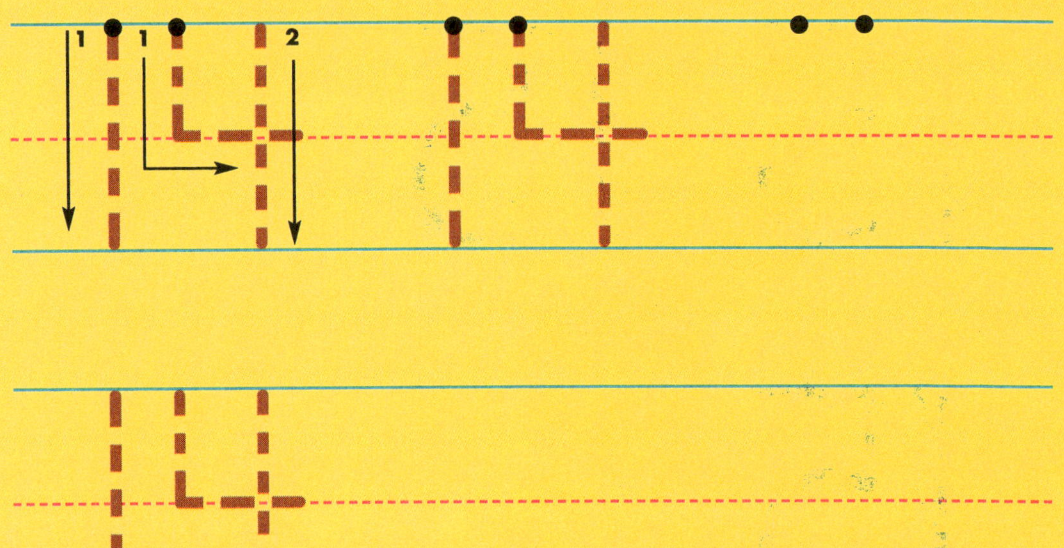

Fifteen 15

Trace and write the number **15**. Write the missing pool ball numbers.

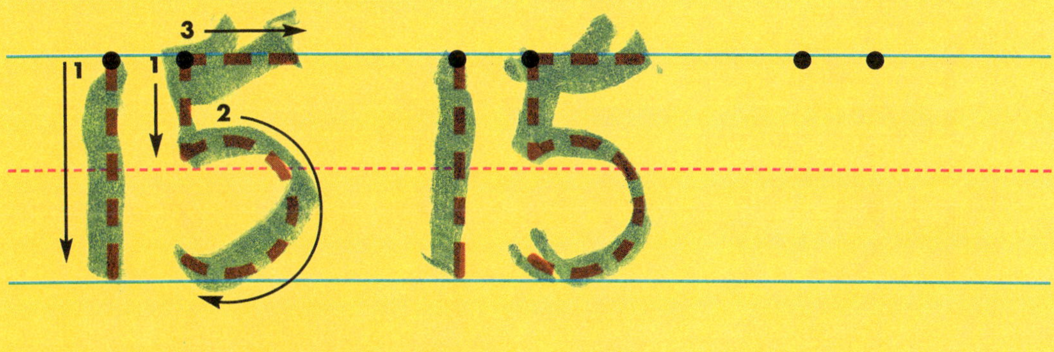

Sixteen 16

Trace and write the number **16**. Draw eight legs on each spider.

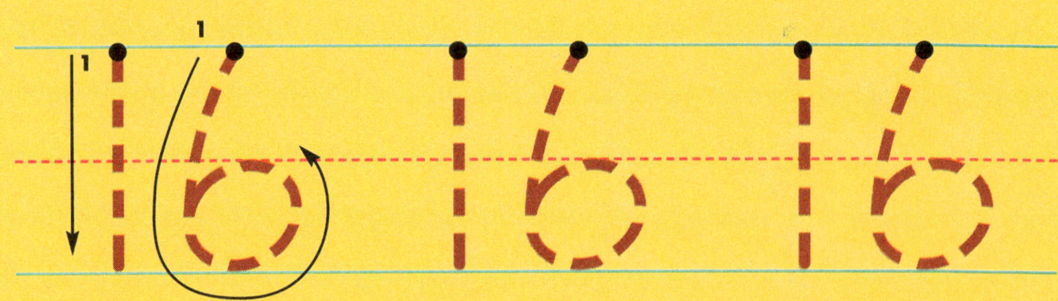

How many legs are there in all? ______________

Seventeen 17

Trace and write the number **17**. Circle each group of **17** things. Color the dog.

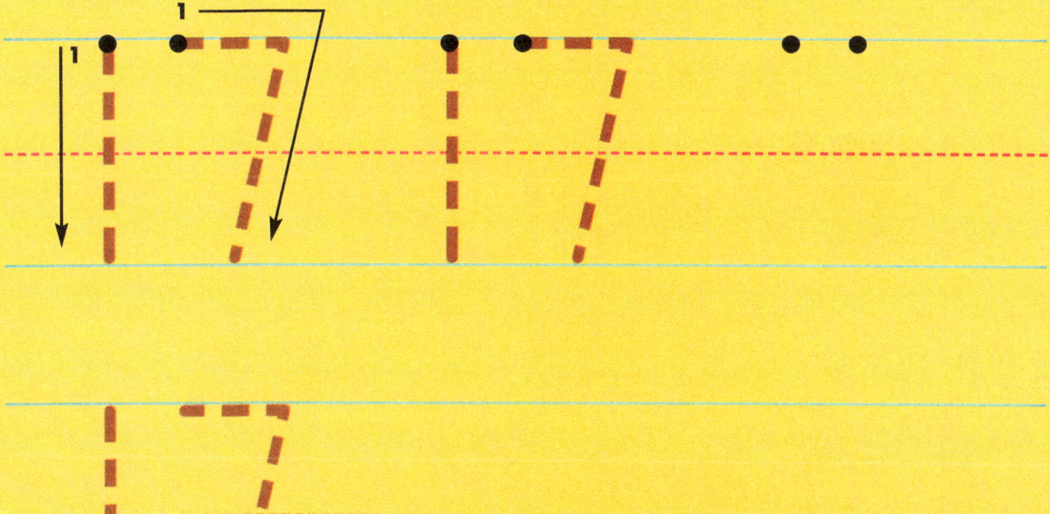

Eighteen 18

Trace and write the number **18**. Help Filbert Fish find his way to the top. Write the numbers **1–18** in each bubble along the way.

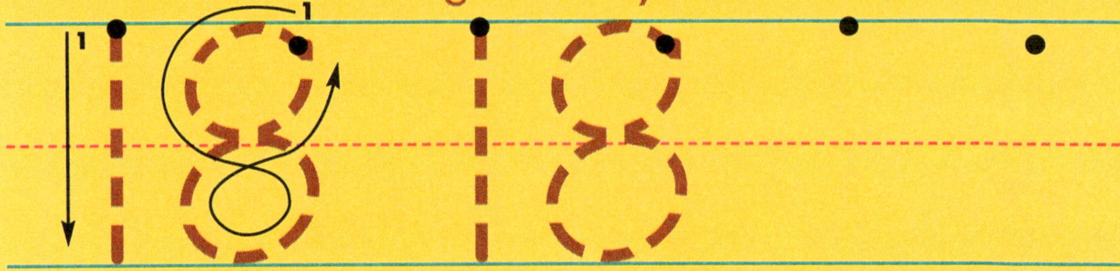

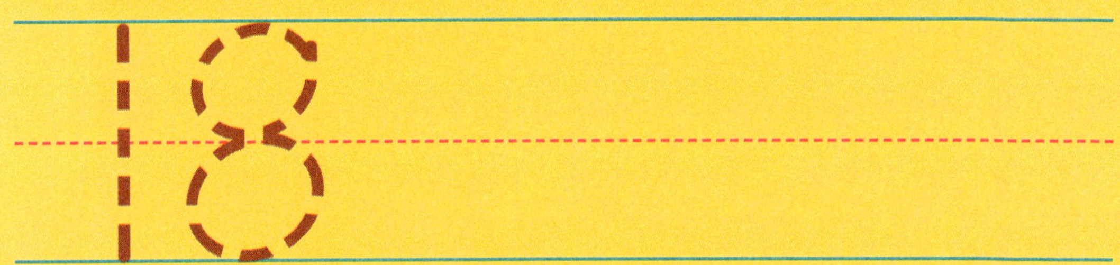

Nineteen 19

Trace and write the number **19**. Circle the numbers **1–19** in the picture.

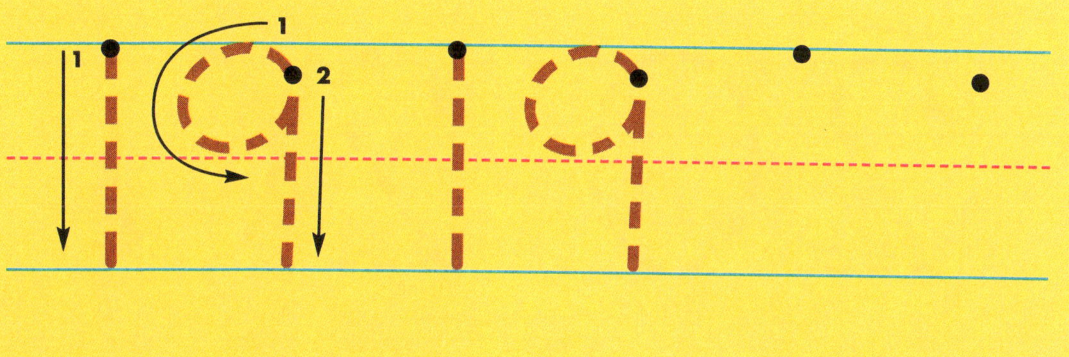

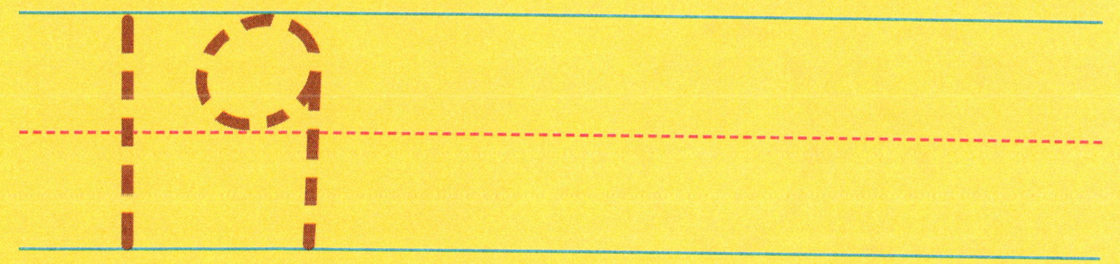

Twenty 20

Trace and write the number **20**. Connect the dots to find the hidden picture.

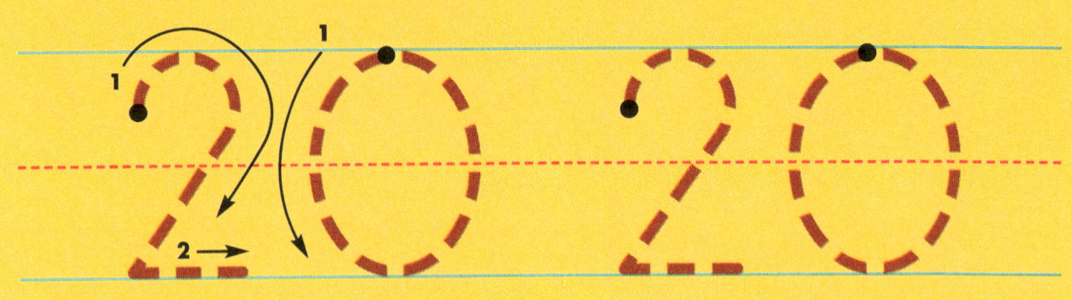

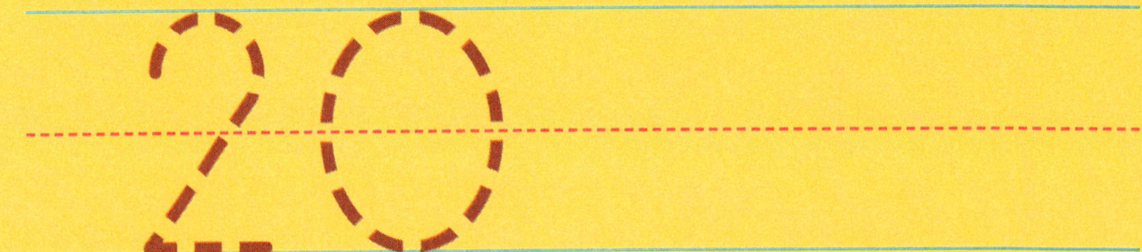

Time for Fun!

Trace the numbers **1–12** in order on the clock.

Hickory Dickory Dock,
The mouse ran up the clock.
The clock struck one and down he ran.
Hickory Dickory Dock.

Time Flies

Write the time that is on each clock.

_______ o'clock

_______ o'clock

_______ o'clock

_______ o'clock

Time Flies

Write the time that is on each clock.

_______ o'clock

_______ o'clock

_______ o'clock

_______ o'clock

Penny Power

A **penny** is worth **1¢**. It is brown. Circle the correct amount of money in each row below.

Give Me Five!

A **nickel** is worth **5¢**. It is silver. Circle the correct amount of money in each row below.

Example:

Time for Dimes

A **dime** is worth **10¢**. It is silver. Circle the correct amount of money in each row below.

Example:

1¢
5¢
10¢

5¢
7¢
10¢

8¢
9¢
10¢

Review Money

Match the price of the thing to the correct amount of money.

Review Money

Match the coins to the correct amount of money.

Get In Shape

Draw and color the shape that comes next in each pattern.

Get In Shape

Draw and color the shape that comes next in each pattern.

Shape Up!

Count the shapes in the picture. Then, complete the graph below.

8				
7				
6				
5				
4				
3				
2				
1				

Shape Up!

Look at the graph on page 201. Then, answer the questions below.

How many **triangles** are there? ______________

How many **rectangles** are there? ____________

How many **octagons** are there? ______________

How many **trapezoids** are there? _____________

Which two shapes are there the same number of?

___________________ and ___________________

How many shapes are there all together? ______

What's for Dinner?

Look at the graph below. Then, answer the questions on page 204.

What's for Dinner?

Answer the questions about the graph on page 203.

How many people like hot dogs best? __________

How many people like pizza best? __________

How many people like chicken best? __________

Which food do most people like best? __________

Which two foods do the same number of people like best ?

__________________ and __________________

Which food do the fewest number of people like best?

____

Find Your Way Home

Read the clues below. Draw an **X** on the houses that do not fit the clues. Circle the correct house.

The house is **white**.
The house has a **red** door.
The house has a fence in front of it.

Rain, Rain, Go Away

Read the clues below. Draw an **X** on the umbrellas that do not fit the clues. Circle the correct umbrella.

The umbrella is open.
The umbrella is big.
The umbrella has dots on it.

Going for a Ride

Read the clues below. Draw an **X** on the bicycles that do not fit the clues. Circle the correct bicycle.

The bicycle has a bell.
The bicycle is **blue**.
The bicycle has a flat tire.

Number Detective

Read the clues below. Draw an **X** on the numbers that do not fit the clues. Circle the correct number.

The number is **less** than **7**.
The number is **greater** than **2**.
The number **equals 3** + **1**.

8 3

1

- **ABC Order:** Putting letters or words in the order in which they appear in the alphabet.
- **Beginning Consonant:** The sound made by the first letter of a word or a picture name.
- **Capital Letters:** Letters that are used at the beginning of names of people and places. They are also used at the beginning of sentences.
- **Consonants:** The letters of the alphabet excluding the five vowels a, e, i, o and u. The consonants are b, c, d, f, g, h, j, k, l, m, n, p, q, r, s, t, v, w, x, y, and z.
- **Ending Consonant:** The sound made by the last letter of a word or a picture name.
- **Graphing:** Using a diagram to show the relationship between two or more sets of objects with pictures.
- **Lowercase letters:** The letters which are often called "small" letters. They are the letters a, b, c, d, e, f, g, h, i, j, k, l, m, n, o, p, q, r, s, t, u, v, w, x, y, and z.
- **Measuring:** The process of determining the size, quantity or amount of something.
- **Opposites:** Things that are different in every way.

- **Ordinal Numbers:** Numbers that show order in a series, such as first, second, or third.
- **Patterns:** Recognizing a series of shapes or designs that are similar to a given one.
- **Rhyme:** Words with the same ending sound.
- **Riddles:** Questions in which clues to an answer are provided.
- **Sequencing:** Putting things in logical order.
- **Short Vowels:** The letters a, e, i, o, and u. Short vowel a is the sound heard in cat; short vowel e is the sound heard in hen; short vowel i is the sound heard in pig; short vowel o is the sound heard in fox; short vowel u is the sound heard in tub.
- **Thinking Skills:** Problem solving skills, such as deductive reasoning, classifying, making inferences, comparing, brainstorming, etc. that enable people to think creatively and logically.
- **Uppercase letters:** The letters of the alphabet which are called "capital" letters. They are A, B, C, D, E, F, G, H, I, J, K, L, M, N, O, P, Q, R, S, T, U, V, W, X, Y, and Z.
- **Word Recognition:** The ability to read or recognize words.

TEACHING SUGGESTIONS

Basic Skills

- Write your child's name on a sheet of paper. Then, have your child trace over it with different colored markers to make a rainbow effect.

  Michael

- Create "name art" with your child. Have your child write his/her name on a sheet of paper and illustrate it.
- Help your child learn his/her full name, address and telephone number. Explain situations when it is important for your child to be able to provide this information.
- Sing and dance the "Hokey Pokey" with your child to practice the concepts of left and right.
- Discuss types of weather. Ask your child to identify the clothes that he/she would wear when the weather is rainy, snowy, hot, etc.
- Look at family pictures with your child. Discuss some of the things that are the same about family members as well as some of the things that make them unique individuals.

- Talk with your child about foods he/she likes to eat. Talk about why they are good for you and where they come from. Help your child understand where foods come from before they go to the grocery store. Group foods by food group: fruits, vegetables, sweets, grains, etc.

- Find pictures of animals and have your child name them. Help your child learn the names for the animal babies and the sounds the animals make.
- Talk about the importance of trees to our environment (homes for animals, food, shade, clean air). You may want to read the book *A Tree Is Nice* by Janet May Udry.
- Plant seeds with your child and keep a record of what happens. Talk about the order in which the changes occur.
- Make a chart with your child that lists his/her daily routine. For example: *8 o'clock—time to get up.* Talk about the sequence in which he/she does things.
- Have a "Things That Go Together" scavenger hunt. Make a list of things found around the house that need "partners" (or use the objects themselves) and have your child search the house for them. For example: *A toothbrush needs __________. Peanut butter needs ____________.*
- Play a color search game. Ask your child to find as many things as he/she can that are the color you name.
- Buy fingerpaints and allow your child to experiment, mixing them to make other colors.
- Bake a cake or make cutout cookies with your child and allow him/her to mix food coloring into white frosting to create different colors of frosting.
- Set out an assortment of dried beans. Have your child sort them into piles by shape, size, and color.

- Take a walk with your child and encourage him/her to pick up "treasures" along the way. After returning home, ask your child how he/she could sort the treasures into groups and have him/her do so.
- Have your child put away the silverware. Have him/her sort the forks, knives, small spoons, and large spoons.
- Have your child organize his/her clothes by type or color.
- Talk with your child about ways his/her toys and books could be organized by how they are alike in color, size, etc.
- Play "Mommy or Daddy Says" the same way "Simon Says" is played. Give your child verbal directions. He/she is only to follow them if preceded by the words "Mommy Says" or "Daddy Says."
- Give your child directions in three or four steps. Say them clearly and in order, holding up a finger as you say each one. See how well your child can remember your directions and follow them.
- Look for shapes around the house. Make a list of things that are circles, squares, rectangles and triangles.

Squares	Circles

- Make a geoboard for your child. Pound equally spaced rows of nails into a square piece of wood. Using rubber bands, have your child create different shapes on the geoboard.
- Help your child observe shapes in nature. Take a walk and collect leaves, seeds, nuts, stones, etc. Have your child sort them into groups by shape, then by color and size.

- Find opportunities around the house to compare things that are big and small. Have your child compare objects, focusing on their size.
- Have your child trace your hand. Then, have your child trace his/her own hand and compare the sizes. Whose hand is bigger? Whose is smaller? Who has longer fingers? Whose fingers are shorter?
- Have your child use paper clips to measure things around the house. Challenge him/her to think of other units that could be used to measure (spoons, pencils, etc.).
- Take out different-sized glasses and cups. Let your child experiment filling and emptying them. Talk to your child about the concepts of full and empty.
- While experimenting with the cups, help your child count the number of times you must pour liquid from a small cup to fill a larger one. Talk about the relationship between sizes.
- Have your child make a bead necklace using a pattern that he/she develops. Check to be sure there is consistency throughout the pattern.
- Lay similar objects on the table in a pattern and have your child identify the pattern.

- Set objects on, below and between each other on the kitchen table. Ask your child where the objects are located. Have your child move the objects and quiz you!

Reading

- Read to and with your child every day to foster a lifelong love of books and reading. Let your child sit on your lap or beside you so that he/she can see the pictures as you read. Point to the words you read, and if there are repeated refrains in the books you read, pause at those points and let your child supply the words.

- Be sure your child sees you reading. Let him/her know how important reading is in your life, both at home and on the job.
- Call attention to the pictures in the books you read and talk about them with your child.
- Stop as you are reading a story and ask your child what he/she thinks will happen next.
- Talk to your child about the characters in the stories and the setting.
- Talk about the sequence of the story. Have your child tell you what happened first, in the middle, and at the end.

- Help your child understand that print has meaning by encouraging him/her to "read" cereal boxes and other print around the house.
- Look for print on street and business signs and have your child "read" it. Explain what these signs mean and why they are important.
- Encourage your child to point out letters he/she recognizes in print and practice spelling words he/she sees frequently. Use magazines, newspapers, and coloring books to help your child create letter and word collages.
- Label objects around the house so that your child will learn to associate the object with the printed word. Index cards written with colored markers work well.
- Focus on a "letter of the day" (or week) in your home. Help your child look for that letter in print and think of words that begin with that letter.

- Create a chart labeled with color words. Go through magazines with your child and let him/her find pictures that are that color, gluing them on the correct section of the chart.
- Go through the grocery ads and have your child cut out the pictures and words. Play a matching game.

- Buy magnetic letters and put them on the refrigerator. Encourage your child to spell words with them.
- Create your own ABC book or list of words your child can write. Let your child illustrate the book.
- Play "I Spy" with your child. ("I spy something that begins with the letter A.") Have your child guess what it is.
- Play "I'm Thinking of a Letter." Give your child different clues about a letter. See how many clues it takes for him/her to guess it. Then have your child think of a letter for you to guess.
- Have your child shape cooked spaghetti into each of the letters of the alphabet. He/she could then make objects that begin with each letter.
- Give your child old magazines. Give him/her directions such as "Circle all the m's." Continue with various directions, making sure to include different letters of the alphabet.

- Make sugar cookie dough and have your child form letters and words with the dough. Then, bake the letters and let your child eat his/her favorite words. Don't forget to have him/her say the sound the letter makes as he/she eats it.

- Go through photo albums and let your child select a picture from each year of his/her life. Help your child sequence them. He/she may want to write his/her age or a brief caption underneath each picture.
- Encourage relatives or friends to send postcards or special occasion cards to your child to encourage him/her to read.
- Make frequent trips to the library and let your child explore the books there, choosing some favorites to take home for you to read.

- Ask grandparents, other family members or friends to recommend books that they liked as a child and have them tell your child why they liked them.
- Arrange a book swap with families of other young children so the children can read their friends' favorite books.
- Have your child dictate a story using greeting card or magazine pictures. Write the story for your child and help him/her read it.

Writing

- Provide your child with many different writing materials—pens, pencils, markers, crayons, paints—and many kinds of paper—writing paper, greeting cards, postcards, invitations, etc. Encourage your child to write and to draw illustrations.

- Keep your child's writing materials in a special place where they can be used independently.
- Buy a notebook for your child's writing. Let him/her decorate it and make it special. Encourage your child to write in the notebook every day. When your child writes something, provide opportunities for him/her to share it with you.
- When your child draws a picture, have him/her write a caption or dictate a caption for you to write. Be sure to write exactly what your child dictates.
- Encourage your child to help you when you are writing: making grocery lists, writing notes and letters, etc. Talk about how writing is important to you.
- Provide chalk and a chalkboard for your child.
- Spend time writing outdoors with your child. Write with sidewalk chalk all over the driveway.
- Take a trip to the beach with your child and use sticks to write words in the sand. Read what you write to each other.
- Enter art/coloring/writing contests often. This encourages creativity, finished work, and the idea of publishing your child's work.
- Use your computer as a writing tool. Have your child type the alphabet or short messages on the screen. Print out the finished product.

- Make pudding with your child. Spread it on a cookie sheet and let your child write words he/she knows with his/her fingers!
- When on a trip, help your child write postcards home to family and friends.
- Write a book about your child and your family. Use pictures of family members or events. Have your child dictate captions to you or let him/her write them him/herself. Punch holes in the pages and fasten them together.

Math

- Encourage your child to find numbers around the house (clocks, television, telephone, etc.) and tell you how they are used.

- Look for and read numbers as you ride in the car: street signs, house numbers, at gas stations and other businesses, license plate numbers, etc.
- Tell your child how you use numbers in your job and at home.
- Look for numbers in the grocery store. Have your child help you find the prices of items.
- Label different household items with "prices" and play store with your child.

- Capitalize on everyday opportunities to count with your child and to have him/her practice counting. Count cans in the cupboard as you put them away, count books on the bookshelf or toys as they are picked up.
- Have your child listen and identify the number of times that you make a special noise like clapping or snapping your fingers.
- Let your child play counting and number games with blocks. For example, count how many blocks tall you can make a tower before it topples!

- Make number cards from index cards. Write a number from 1 to 20 on each card and have your child practice putting them in order.
- Give your child a number card and a supply of small objects (macaroni, beads, blocks, etc.) and have him/her practice counting the correct number of objects. Let your child practice with many different numbers. Then, count out a number of objects and have your child match the correct number card to it.
- Say a number and have your child tell you what number comes after it or before it.
- Use magazine pictures to make a counting book. Write a number on each page and have your child cut out pictures of that number of objects on the page.

- Find numbers in catalogs and let your child practice reading them.
- Punch ten holes in an old greeting card cover with a nice picture. Number the holes. Give your child a piece of string and have him/her thread the holes in the correct order.
- Sing "This Old Man" with your child, having him/her use fingers to represent the numbers.
- Look for books and songs that incorporate numbers, such as *Ten Sly Piranhas* by William Wise.
- Use the calendar to help your child with number recognition. Talk with your child about the date and month and count the number of days until a special event.
- Place different numbers of objects in an egg carton to give your child practice counting numbers to 12.

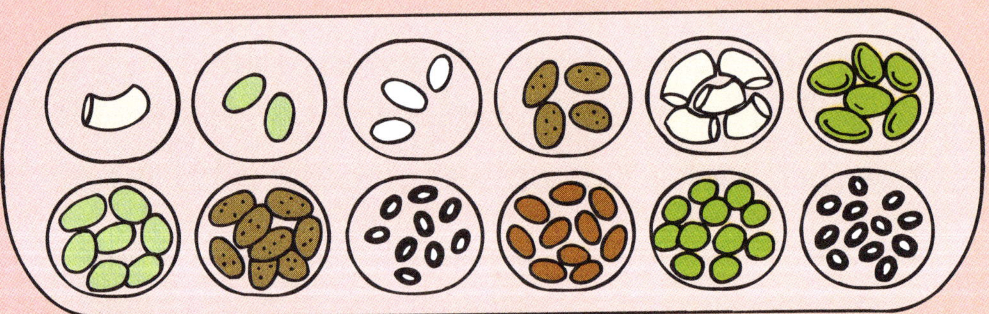

- Number clothespins from 1 to 12. Label index cards with the number words on one side and the corresponding number of dots on the other side. Play a game with your child, having him/her clip the clothespins on the correct card.

- Challenge your child to count back from 10.
- Have your child practice counting by tens. Hold up all ten fingers each time he/she says a number.
- Have your child shape clay into each of the numbers from 1 to 20.
- Draw a number on your child's back with your finger. Have your child tell you what number you drew. Then, let your child draw a number on your back.
- Read *The M&M's Counting Book* by Barbara Barbieri McGrath with your child. Then, do some of the suggested activities.
- Talk with your child about ways he/she helps at home. Ask: How can learning to count help us in setting the table?
- Put out a small pile of coins and have your child practice sorting and naming them. Have pennies, nickels, dimes, and quarters available for your child to manipulate. Have your child count how many there are of each coin and talk about the value of each coin.
- Have your child help set the table. Help him/her use one napkin for each plate, one fork for each napkin, etc.

6
BASIC SKILLS
Red Ahead!
Color each picture red. Then, draw a picture of something else red.
drawings will vary

7
BASIC SKILLS
Go, Go Yellow!
Color each picture yellow. Then, draw a picture of something else yellow.
drawings will vary

8
BASIC SKILLS
What's New, Blue?
Circle the blue picture in each row.

9
BASIC SKILLS
Going Green
Color each picture green. Then, draw a picture of something else green.
drawings will vary

10
BASIC SKILLS
A Slice of Orange
Circle the orange picture in each row.

11
BASIC SKILLS
Purple on Parade
Color each picture purple. Then, draw a picture of something else purple.
GRAPE
JELLY
drawings will vary

12 BASIC SKILLS

Back to Black

Circle the **black** picture in each row.

18
Square Dance
Trace the square below. Then, draw a line under the square in each row.

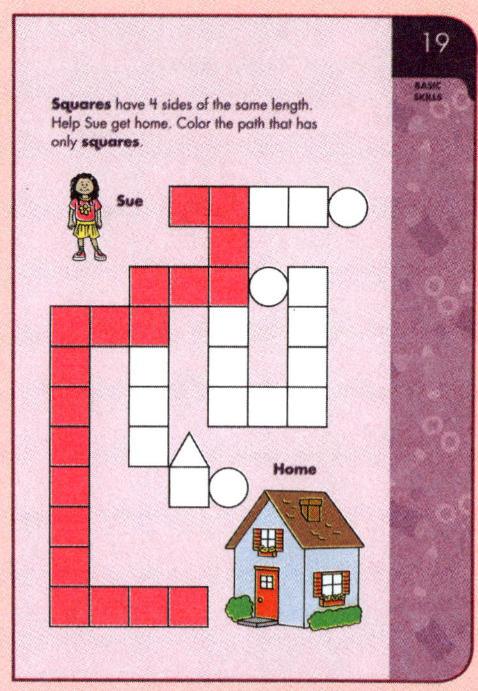
19
Squares have 4 sides of the same length. Help Sue get home. Color the path that has only squares.
Sue
Home

20
Triangle Time
Trace the triangle below. Then, draw a line under the triangle in each row.

21
All triangles have 3 sides. Triangles can be different sizes. Trace and color the triangle shapes below.

22
Rectangles Rule!
Trace the rectangle below. Then, draw a line under the rectangle in each row.

23
All rectangles have 4 sides, but only the opposite sides are the same length. Draw a circle around each picture that has the shape of a rectangle.

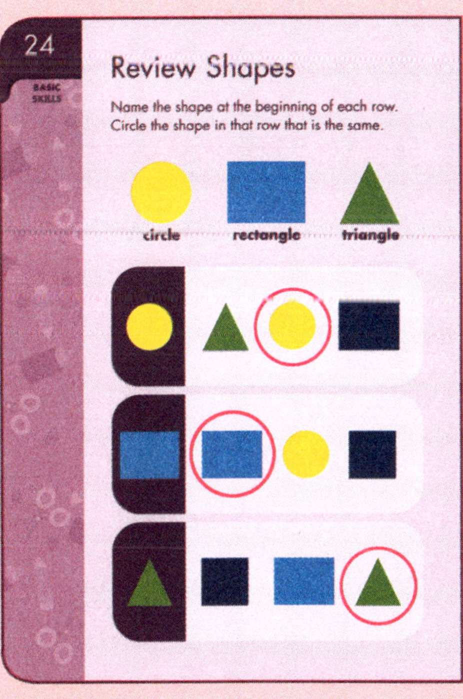
24
BASIC SKILLS
Review Shapes
Name the shape at the beginning of each row. Circle the shape in that row that is the same.
circle
rectangle
triangle

25
BASIC SKILLS
Review Shapes
Color the shapes to complete this picture. Color the squares yellow. Color the triangles red. Color the rectangles green.

26
BASIC SKILLS
Ovals All Over
Trace the oval below. Then, draw a line under the oval in each row.

27
BASIC SKILLS
Draw an X on the pictures that have the shape of an oval.

28
BASIC SKILLS
Diamond Days
Trace the diamond below. Then, draw a line under the diamond in each row.

29
BASIC SKILLS
Help Jim get to the kite shop. Color the path that has only diamonds.
Jim
Kite Shop

30
BASIC SKILLS
A Star Is Born
Trace the **star** below. Then, draw a line under the **star** in each row.

31
BASIC SKILLS
Connect the dots in order to make your own **stars**.
Twinkle, twinkle, little star.
How I wonder what you are.
Up above the world so high,
Like a diamond in the sky.
Twinkle, twinkle, little star.
How I wonder what you are.

32
BASIC SKILLS
Review Shapes
Color the **squares purple**. Color the **triangles blue**. Color the **diamonds yellow**.

33
BASIC SKILLS
Review Shapes
Trace and color each shape. Draw and color two more of each shape.

34
BASIC SKILLS
Simply the Same
Color the shape in each row that looks the same as the first shape.

35
BASIC SKILLS
Dare to Be Different
Draw an **X** on the picture in each group that is different.

36
BASIC SKILLS

All Together Now

Color the pictures in each group that go together.
Draw an **X** on the one that does not belong.

37
BASIC SKILLS

All Together Now

Draw an **X** on the picture that does not belong.
Draw another thing that does belong.

drawings will vary

38
BASIC SKILLS

Opposites Attract

Opposites are things that are different in every way. Draw a line to match the opposites.

day
sad
front
night
happy
back

39
BASIC SKILLS

Opposites Attract

Draw a picture of the opposite.

drawing of a night scene
day
night

drawing of a happy face
sad
happy

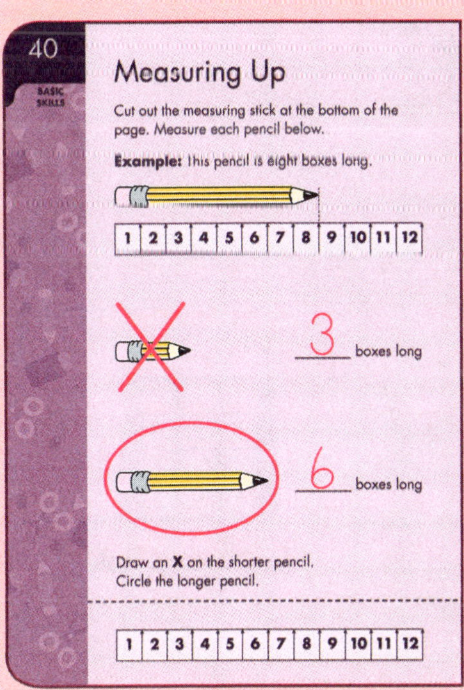
40
BASIC SKILLS

Measuring Up

Cut out the measuring stick at the bottom of the page. Measure each pencil below.

Example: This pencil is eight boxes long.

1	2	3	4	5	6	7	8	9	10	11	12

3 boxes long

6 boxes long

Draw an **X** on the shorter pencil.
Circle the longer pencil.

1	2	3	4	5	6	7	8	9	10	11	12

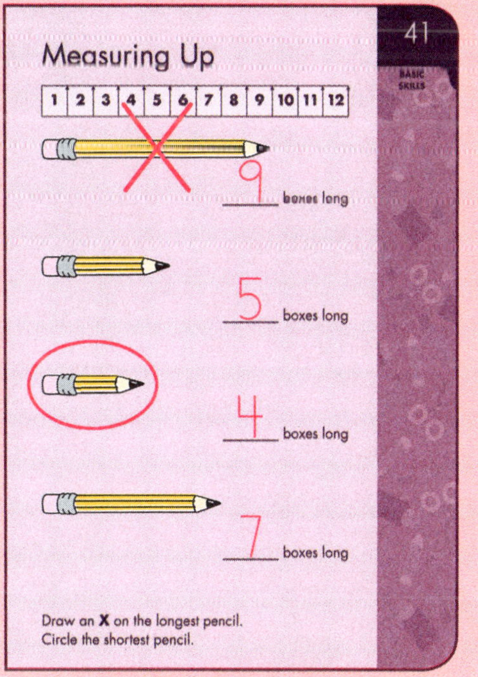
41
BASIC SKILLS

Measuring Up

1	2	3	4	5	6	7	8	9	10	11	12

9 boxes long

5 boxes long

4 boxes long

7 boxes long

Draw an **X** on the longest pencil.
Circle the shortest pencil.

42
BASIC SKILLS
What's Up?
Color the pictures above the clouds first. Then, color the pictures below the clouds

44
WRITING READINESS
Top to Bottom
Draw a line from the top picture to the bottom picture.

45
WRITING READINESS
Snacktime!
Draw a line from the picture on the left to the picture on the right.

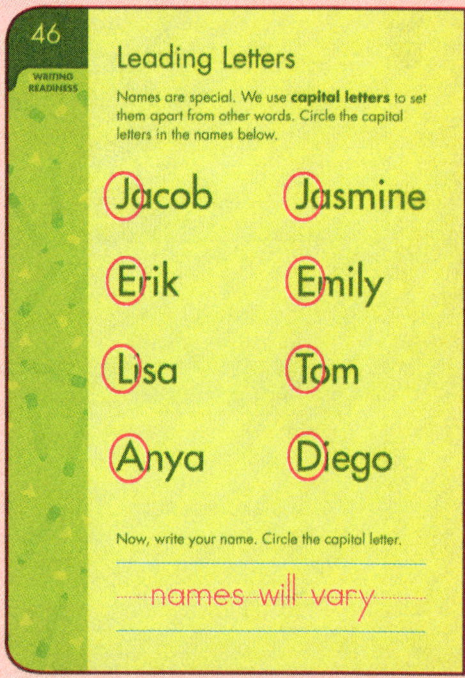
46
WRITING READINESS
Leading Letters
Names are special. We use capital letters to set them apart from other words. Circle the capital letters in the names below.
Jacob
Jasmine
Erik
Emily
Lisa
Tom
Anya
Diego
Now, write your name. Circle the capital letter.
names will vary

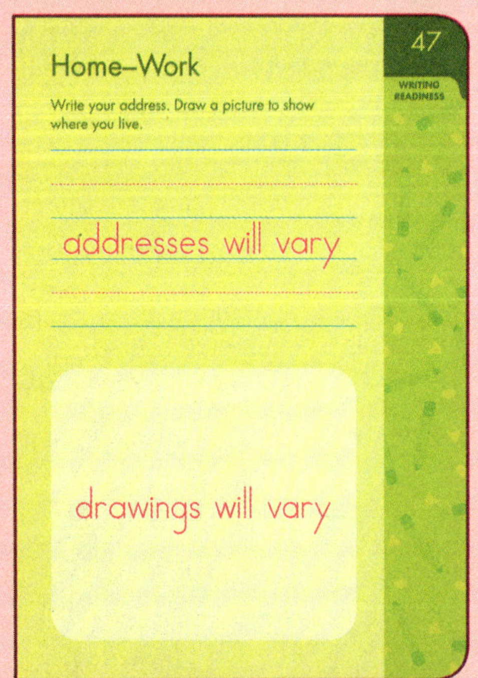
47
WRITING READINESS
Home–Work
Write your address. Draw a picture to show where you live.
addresses will vary
drawings will vary

48
WRITING READINESS
Give Me a Ring!
Write your phone number. Practice dialing it using the phone below.
numbers will vary
Color the numbers in your phone number on the phone above.

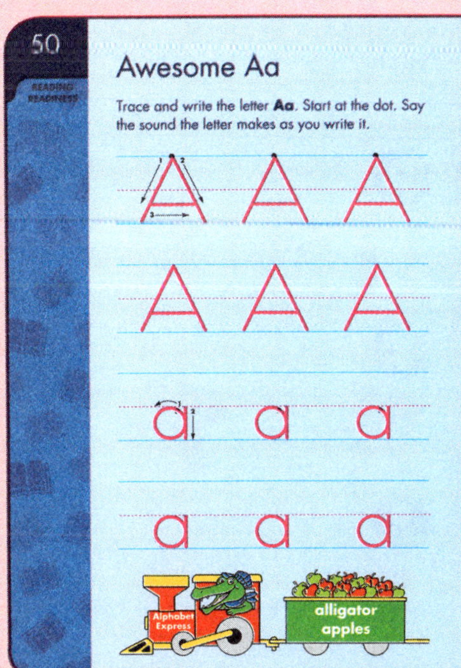
50
Awesome Aa
Trace and write the letter Aa. Start at the dot. Say the sound the letter makes as you write it.
Alphabet Express
alligator apples

51
Beautiful Bb
Trace and write the letter Bb. Start at the dot. Say the sound the letter makes as you write it.
bear
balls

52
Classy Cc
Trace and write the letter Cc. Start at the dot. Say the sound the letter makes as you write it.
cats
cookies

53
Review Aa, Bb, Cc
Look at the letter each insect is holding. Circle the same letter below.
A a
V X A o a c
B b
R B F g b k
C c
O Q C f a c

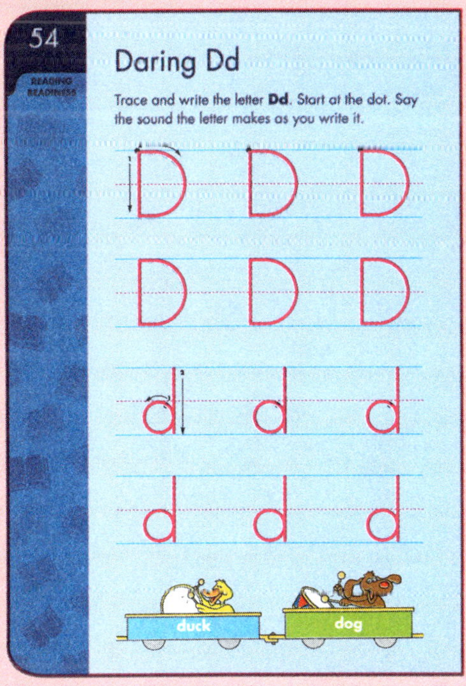
54
Daring Dd
Trace and write the letter Dd. Start at the dot. Say the sound the letter makes as you write it.
duck
dog

55
Excellent Ee
Trace and write the letter Ee. Start at the dot. Say the sound the letter makes as you write it.
elephant
eggs

56
READING READINESS
Fantastic Ff
Trace and write the letter **Ff**. Start at the dot. Say the sound the letter makes as you write it.
frog
fish

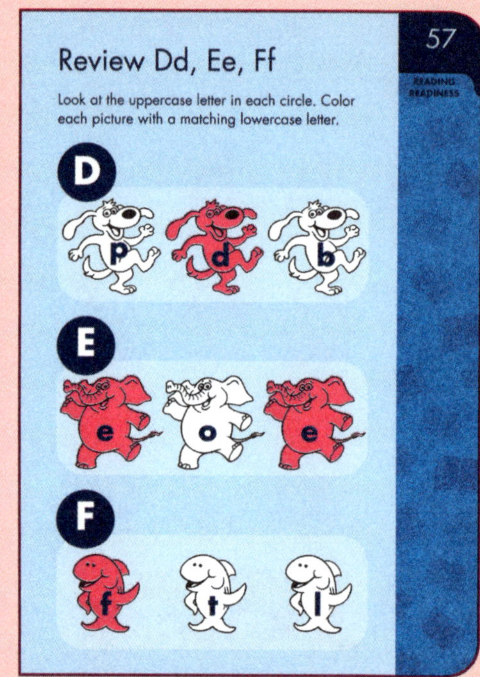
57
READING READINESS
Review Dd, Ee, Ff
Look at the uppercase letter in each circle. Color each picture with a matching lowercase letter.
D
p
d
b
E
e
o
e
F
f
t
l

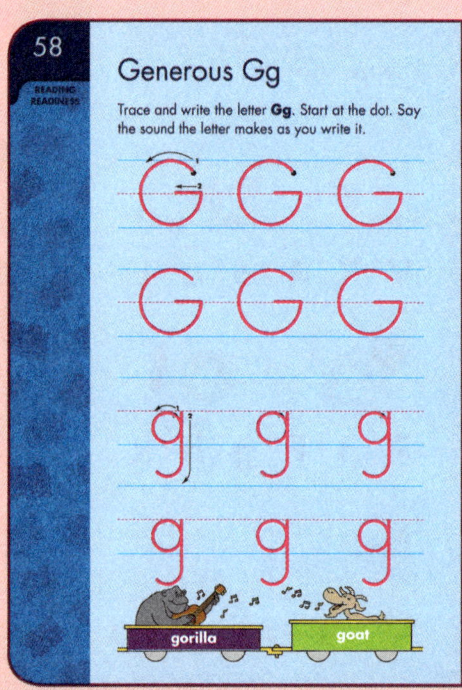
58
READING READINESS
Generous Gg
Trace and write the letter **Gg**. Start at the dot. Say the sound the letter makes as you write it.
gorilla
goat

59
READING READINESS
Honest Hh
Trace and write the letter **Hh**. Start at the dot. Say the sound the letter makes as you write it.
hippo
hats

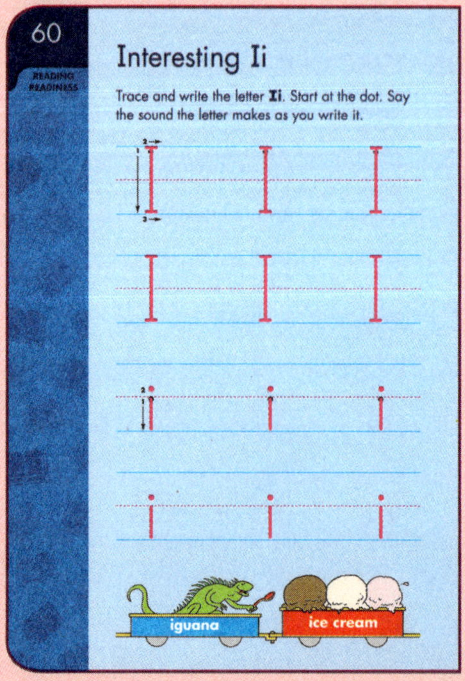
60
READING READINESS
Interesting Ii
Trace and write the letter **Ii**. Start at the dot. Say the sound the letter makes as you write it.
iguana
ice cream

61
READING READINESS
Review Gg, Hh, Ii
Draw a line from each uppercase letter to its matching lowercase letter.
Gg Hh Ii
H
g
G
I
i
h

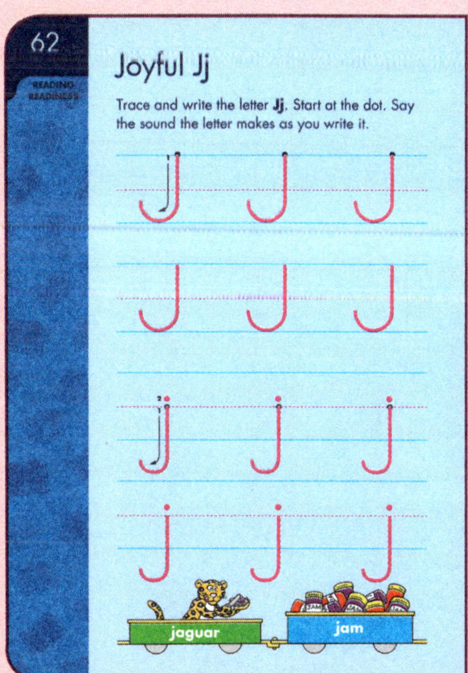
62
READING READINESS
Joyful Jj
Trace and write the letter Jj. Start at the dot. Say the sound the letter makes as you write it.
jaguar
jam

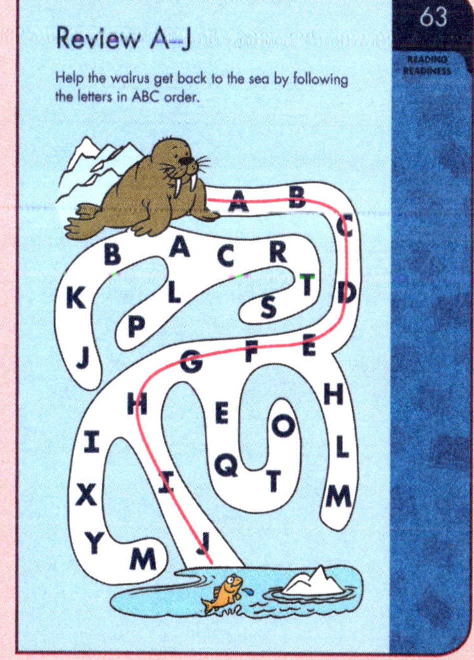
63
READING READINESS
Review A–J
Help the walrus get back to the sea by following the letters in ABC order.

64
READING READINESS
Kindly Kk
Trace and write the letter Kk. Start at the dot. Say the sound the letter makes as you write it.
kangaroo
keys

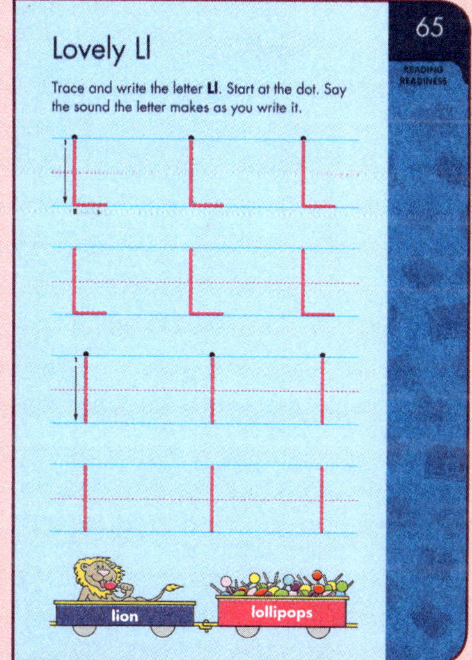
65
READING READINESS
Lovely Ll
Trace and write the letter Ll. Start at the dot. Say the sound the letter makes as you write it.
lion
lollipops

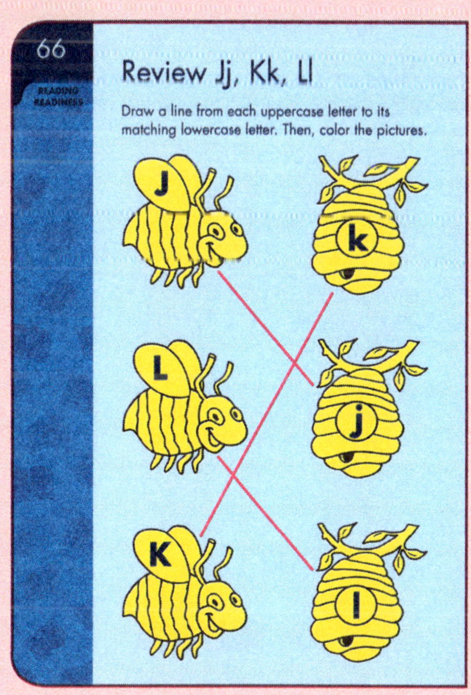
66
READING READINESS
Review Jj, Kk, Ll
Draw a line from each uppercase letter to its matching lowercase letter. Then, color the pictures.

67
READING READINESS
Mighty Mm
Trace and write the letter Mm. Start at the dot. Say the sound the letter makes as you write it.
monkey
money

68
READING READINESS
Review Aa–Mm
Help Adam get to the playground. Follow the letters in ABC order.
Aa
Bb
Cc
Bb
Dd
Ee
Ff
Ff
Ll
Gg
Hh
Kk
Ii
Jj
Kk
Ll
Jj
Mm
Kk

69
READING READINESS
Nifty Nn
Trace and write the letter **Nn**. Start at the dot. Say the sound the letter makes as you write it.
newt
nest

70
READING READINESS
Ordinary Oo
Trace and write the letter **Oo**. Start at the dot. Say the sound the letter makes as you write it.
ostrich
octopus

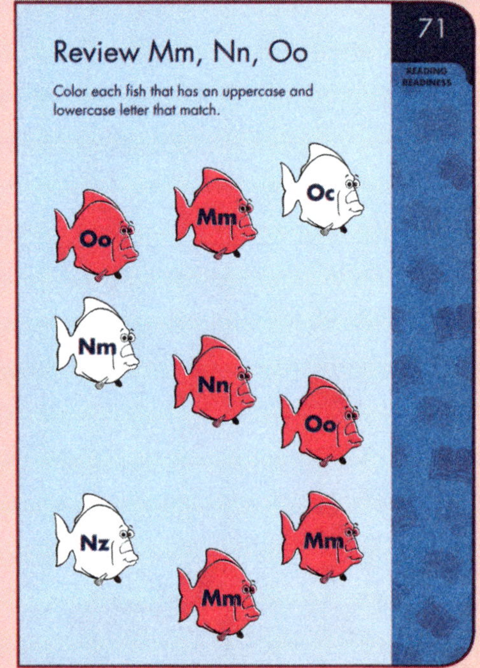
71
READING READINESS
Review Mm, Nn, Oo
Color each fish that has an uppercase and lowercase letter that match.
Oo
Mm
Oc
Nm
Nn
Oo
Nz
Mm
Mm

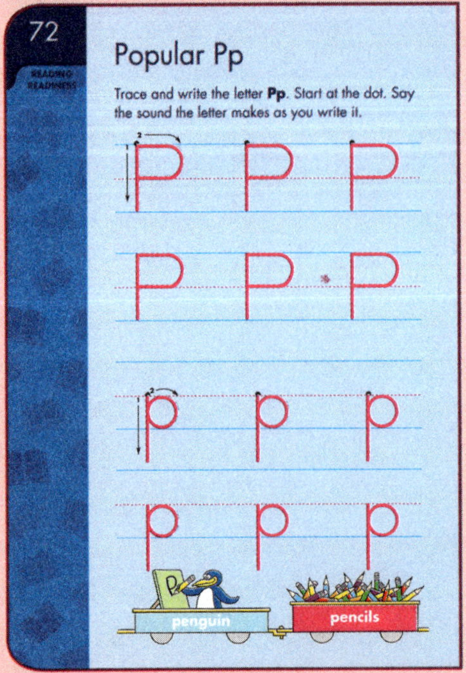
72
READING READINESS
Popular Pp
Trace and write the letter **Pp**. Start at the dot. Say the sound the letter makes as you write it.
penguin
pencils

73
READING READINESS
Quiet Qq
Trace and write the letter **Qq**. Start at the dot. Say the sound the letter makes as you write it.
quarters
queen

74
Remarkable Rr
Trace and write the letter **Rr**. Start at the dot. Say the sound the letter makes as you write it.
rabbit
rocks

75
Super Ss
Trace and write the letter **Ss**. Start at the dot. Say the sound the letter makes as you write it.
seal
sea horse

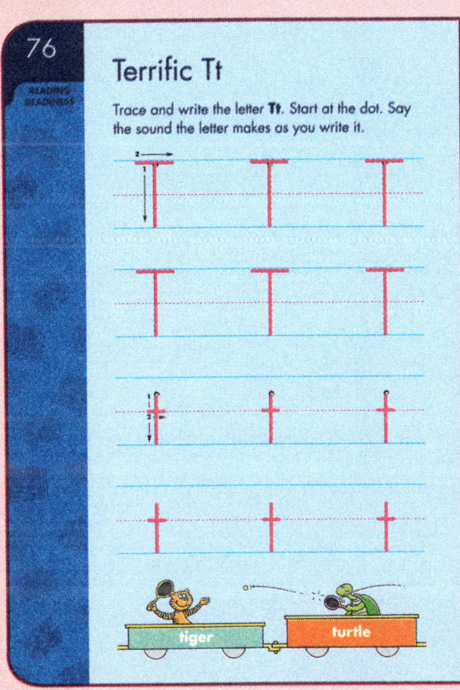
76
Terrific Tt
Trace and write the letter **Tt**. Start at the dot. Say the sound the letter makes as you write it.
tiger
turtle

77
Review Pp–Tt
Draw a line from each uppercase letter to its matching lowercase letter.
P
Q
R
S
T
q
r
p
t
s

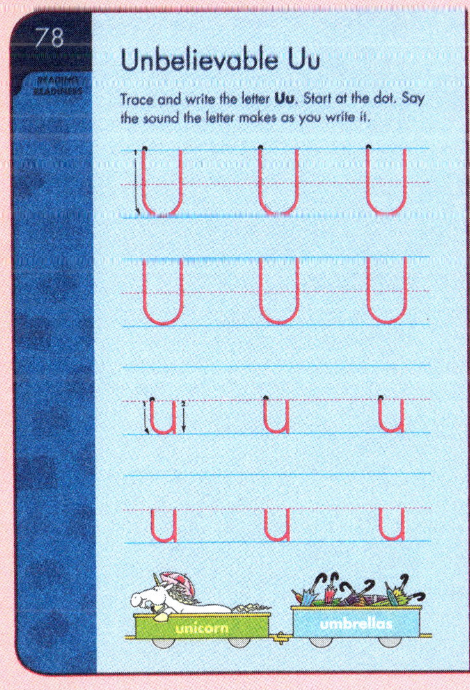
78
Unbelievable Uu
Trace and write the letter **Uu**. Start at the dot. Say the sound the letter makes as you write it.
unicorn
umbrellas

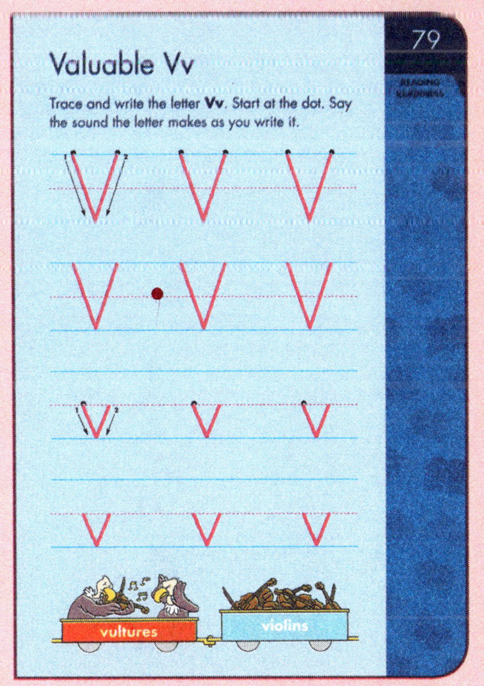
79
Valuable Vv
Trace and write the letter **Vv**. Start at the dot. Say the sound the letter makes as you write it.
vultures
violins

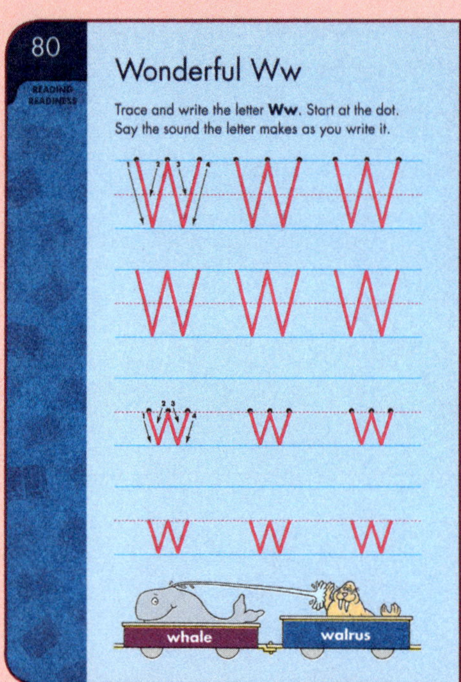
80
Wonderful Ww
Trace and write the letter Ww. Start at the dot. Say the sound the letter makes as you write it.
whale
walrus

81
Exciting Xx
Trace and write the letter Xx. Start at the dot. Say the sound the letter makes as you write it.
x-ray
xylophone

82
Yummy Yy
Trace and write the letter Yy. Start at the dot. Say the sound the letter makes as you write it.
yak
yarn

83
Zippy Zz
Trace and write the letter Zz. Start at the dot. Say the sound the letter makes as you write it.
zippers

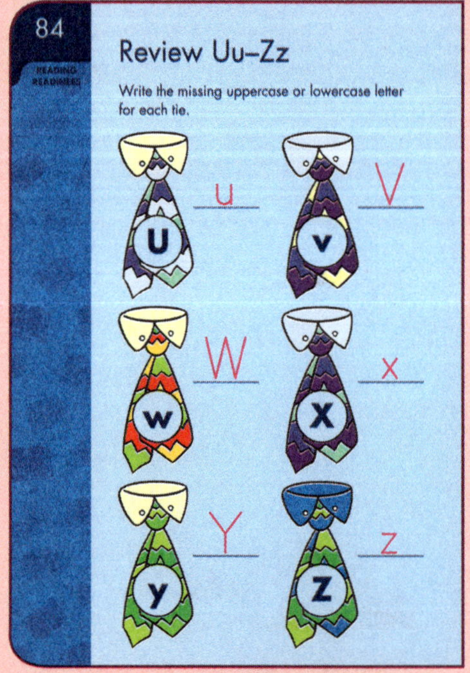
84
Review Uu–Zz
Write the missing uppercase or lowercase letter for each tie.
U u
v V
w W
X x
y Y
Z z

85
Let's Start with ABC
Connect the dots in ABC order. Color the picture.

86

READING READINESS

Review Uppercase Letters

Write the missing uppercase letters to complete the alphabet.

87

READING READINESS

Review Lowercase Letters

Write the missing lowercase letters to complete the alphabet.

88

READING READINESS

Sound Off! Short Aa

Short Aa is the sound at the beginning of the word **alligator**. Color the pictures that begin with the **short Aa** sound.

89

READING READINESS

Sound Off! Short Aa

Say each picture name. Write **a** to complete each word below.

map cat

can fan

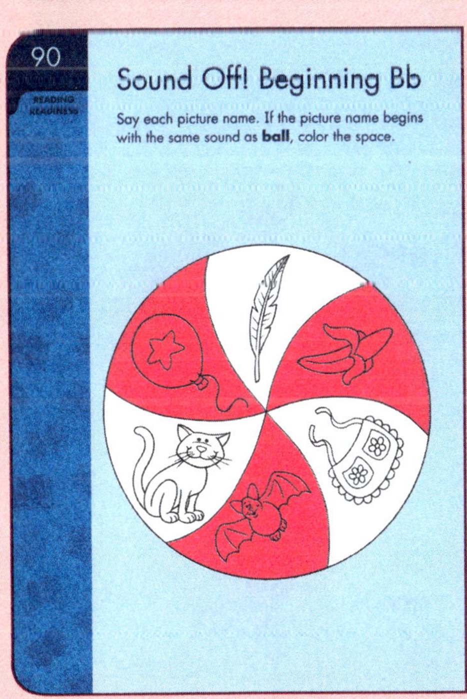
90

READING READINESS

Sound Off! Beginning Bb

Say each picture name. If the picture name begins with the same sound as **ball**, color the space.

91

READING READINESS

Sound Off! Beginning Cc

These pictures begin with the letter **Cc**. Color these pictures.

cat

coat

car

92
Sound Off! Beginning Dd
Say the picture names in each box on the door. Circle the picture whose name begins with the same sound as **dinosaur**.

93
Beginning Bb, Cc, Dd
Look at each picture. Write the letter for the beginning sound under each picture.
d
c
c
b

94
Sound Off! Short Ee
These pictures begin with the letter **Ee**. Color these pictures.
elephant
eggs
envelope

95
Sound Off! Short Ee
Say the name of each picture. Write the letter **e** to complete each word below.
10
ten
bed
sled
fence

96
Sound Off! Beginning Ff
Say each picture name. If the picture name begins with the same sound as **flower**, color the picture.

97
Sound Off! Beginning Gg
These pictures begin with the letter **Gg**. Color these pictures.
goose
girl
goat

98

Sound Off! Beginning Hh

These pictures begin with the letter **Hh**. Color these pictures.

house

hat

horse

99

Beginning Ff, Gg, Hh

Say the sound the letters make. Circle the pictures in each row that begin with the letter shown.

Ff

Gg

Hh

100

Sound Off! Short Ii

Short Ii is the sound at the beginning of the word **igloo**. Color the pictures that begin with the **short Ii** sound.

101

Sound Off! Short Ii

Short Ii is the sound you hear in the middle of the word **pig**. Say each picture name. Write **i** to complete each word below.

chick gift

pin wig

102

Beginning Gg, Hh, Ii

Say the sound the letters make. Circle the pictures in each row that begin with the letter shown.

Gg

Gg

Hh

Hh

Ii

Ii

103

Sounds Off! Beginning Jj

What is Jamie wearing today? Say each picture name. Color the spaces with the **Jj** sound blue. Color the other spaces yellow.

What is Jamie wearing? jeans

104
Sound Off! Beginning Kk
Look at the pictures on the kite's tail. Say each picture name. If the picture begins with the same sound as kite, color it orange. Then, color the kite.

105
Sound Off! Beginning Ll
Cut out the stamps at the bottom of the page. Say each picture name. If the picture begins with the same sound as letter, glue it on an envelope.

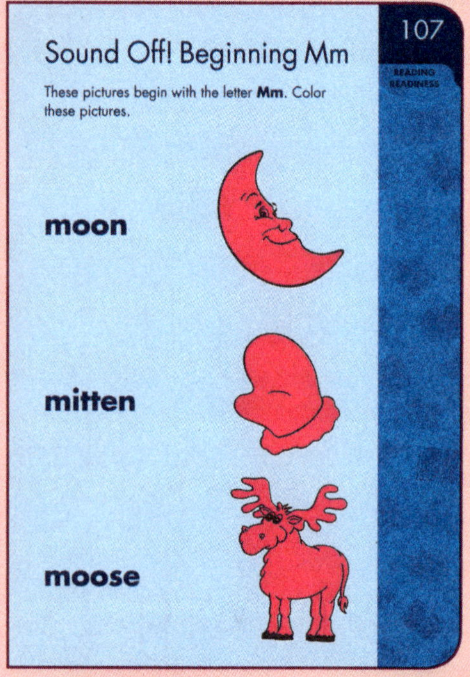
107
Sound Off! Beginning Mm
These pictures begin with the letter Mm. Color these pictures.
moon
mitten
moose

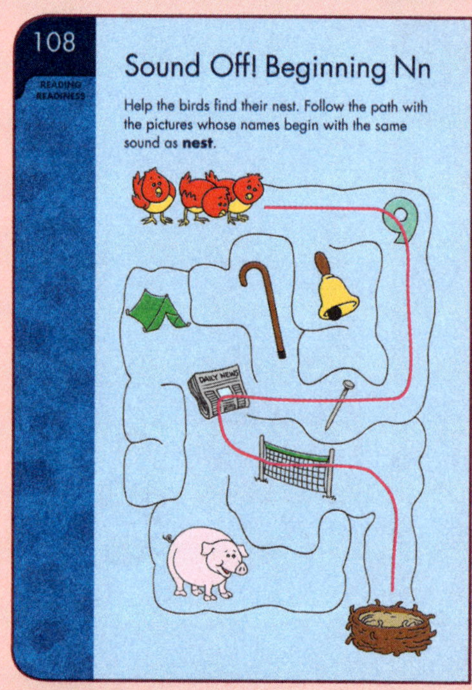
108
Sound Off! Beginning Nn
Help the birds find their nest. Follow the path with the pictures whose names begin with the same sound as nest.

109
Sound Off! Short Oo
Look at the pictures. Color the pictures that begin with the short Oo sound.

110
Sound Off! Short Oo
Say each picture name. Write o to complete each word below.
rock
pot
ox
lock

111
READING READINESS
Review Short Vowels
Say each picture name. Cut out the words. Glue each word where it belongs.
hen
pot
hat
fin
mat

113
READING READINESS
Beginning Mm, Nn, Oo
Say the sound the letters make. Circle the pictures in each row that begin with the letter shown.
Mm
Mm
Nn
Nn
Oo
Oo

114
READING READINESS
Sound Off! Beginning Pp
Pam only packs things whose names begin with the same sound as panda. Say the picture names. Circle each picture whose name begins with the same sound as Pam and panda.

115
READING READINESS
Sound Off! Beginning Qq
These pictures begin with the letter Qq. Color these pictures.
queen
quail
quilt

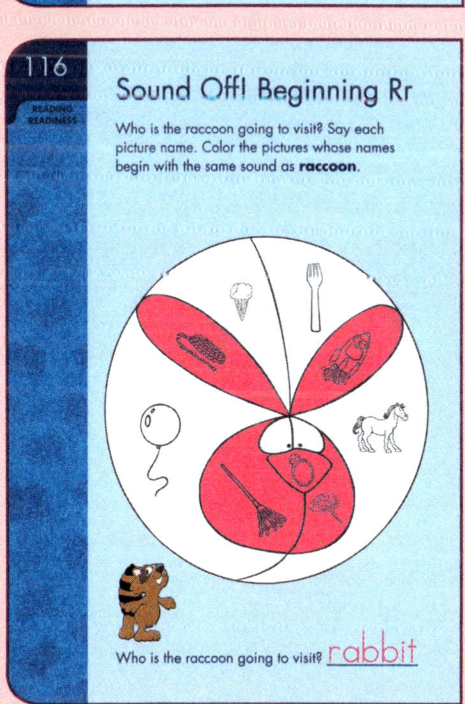
116
READING READINESS
Sound Off! Beginning Rr
Who is the raccoon going to visit? Say each picture name. Color the pictures whose names begin with the same sound as raccoon.
Who is the raccoon going to visit? rabbit

117
READING READINESS
Beginning Pp, Qq, Rr
Say the sound the letters make. Circle the pictures in each row that begin with the letter shown.
Pp
Pp
Qq
Qq
Rr
Rr

118

Beginning Qq, Rr, Ss

Say each picture name. Say the letters. Draw a line from each picture to its matching letter.

Qq

Rr

Ss

119

Sound Off! Beginning Tt

These pictures begin with the letter **Tt**. Color these pictures.

turtle

tie

table

120

Sound Off! Short Uu

Short Uu is the sound you hear in the middle of the word **bug**. Help the bug get to the leaf. Follow the path with the pictures whose names have the **short Uu** sound.

121

Sound Off! Short Uu

Short Uu is the sound you hear in the middle of the word **bus**. Say each picture name. Write **u** to complete each word below.

bus hug

truck mud

122

Beginning Ss, Tt, Uu

Say the sound the letters make. Circle the pictures in each row that begin with the letter shown.

Ss

Ss

Tt

Tt

Uu

Uu

123

Sound Off! Beginning Vv

Cut out the pictures at the bottom of the page. Say each picture name. If the picture begins with the same sound as **van**, glue it on the van.

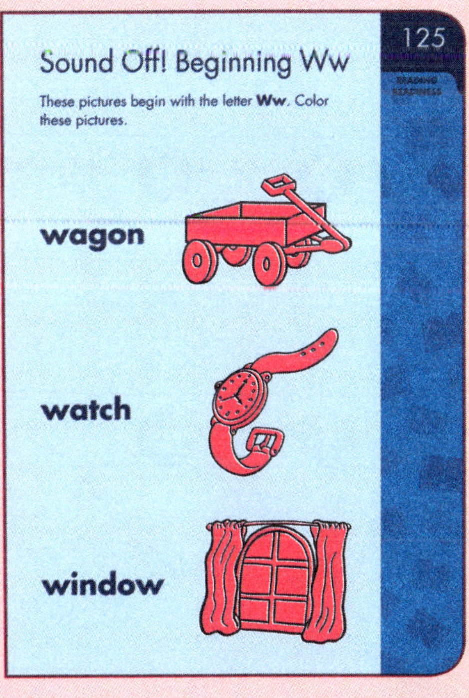
125
Sound Off! Beginning Ww
These pictures begin with the letter Ww. Color these pictures.
wagon
watch
window

126
Sound Off! Consonant Xx
Write an x on the lines to complete each picture name.
EXIT
exit
x-ray
box
fox

127
Beginning Vv, Ww, Xx
Say the sound the letters make. Circle the pictures in each row that have the letter shown.
Vv
Vv
Ww
Ww
Xx
Xx

128
Sound Off! Beginning Yy
Say each picture name. Draw a green line from each ball of yarn to the pictures that begin with the Yy sound.

129
Sound Off! Beginning Zz
These pictures begin with the letter Zz. Color these pictures.
zipper
zig zag
zebra

130
Beginning Yy, Zz
Say the sound the letters make. Circle the pictures in each row that begin with the letter shown.
Yy
Yy
Zz
Zz
0

131
Review Beginning Sounds
Say each picture name. Circle the beginning sound.
t p
n c
b t
b c
2
t p
c b

132
Review Beginning Sounds
Look at the letter in each box. Circle the picture that begins with that sound.
g
d
f
m

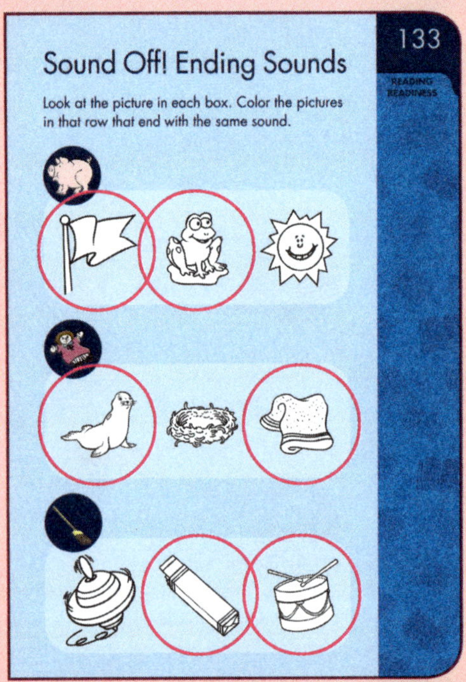
133
Sound Off! Ending Sounds
Look at the picture in each box. Color the pictures in that row that end with the same sound.

134
Sound Off! Ending Sounds
Look at the picture in each box. Circle the ending sound for each picture.
d t
b p
x s
n m
g f
s b

135
Sound Off! Ending Sounds
Say the name of each picture. Write the letter to complete each word.
jar
rug
pig
red

136
Review Short Vowels
Say the name of each picture. Write the letter to complete each word.
cup
pig
dog
pan
ball
bed

137
A-Maze-Ing Vowels
Color your way through the maze by only coloring the vowels. Then, write the five vowels below.
Start
End
a e i o u

138
Rhyme Time
Words that have the same ending sounds are called rhyming words. Circle the pairs that rhyme.
map nest dog frog
hat bat kite mop
can fan mouse pig

139
Rhyme Time
Read the poem. Read the questions. Circle the correct answer.
Jack and Jill went up the hill,
To fetch a pail of water.
Jack fell down and broke his crown,
And Jill came tumbling after.
Who went up the hill?
What were they going to fetch?
Who fell down?

140
Match It: People
Draw a line to match each word with its picture.
boy
girl
man
woman

142
Time for School
What happened first, second and third? Draw a line from the correct word to the picture.
first
second
third

143
Let It Snow!
Cut out the pictures below. Put them in the correct order. Draw what you think will happen next.
drawings will vary

145
MATH READINESS
Order Up!
Color the first leaf red. Circle the third leaf.
Color the fourth balloon purple. Draw a line under the second balloon.

146
MATH READINESS
Follow the Leader
Circle the first thing in each row.

147
MATH READINESS
Line Up!
Circle the last thing in each row.
TICKETS

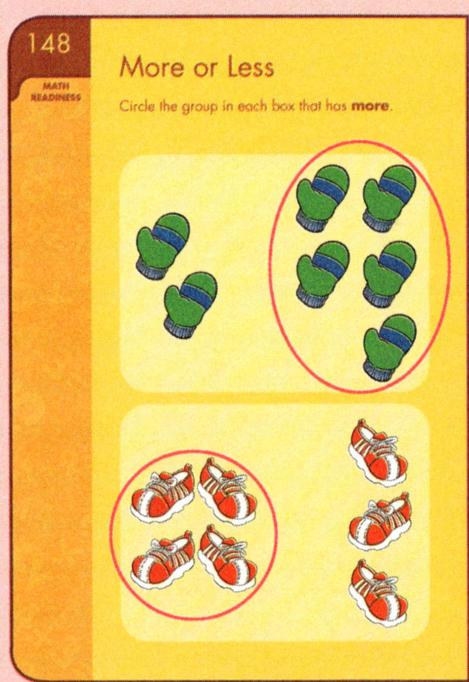
148
MATH READINESS
More or Less
Circle the group in each box that has more.

149
MATH READINESS
Time for Bed!
Circle the group in each box that has fewer.

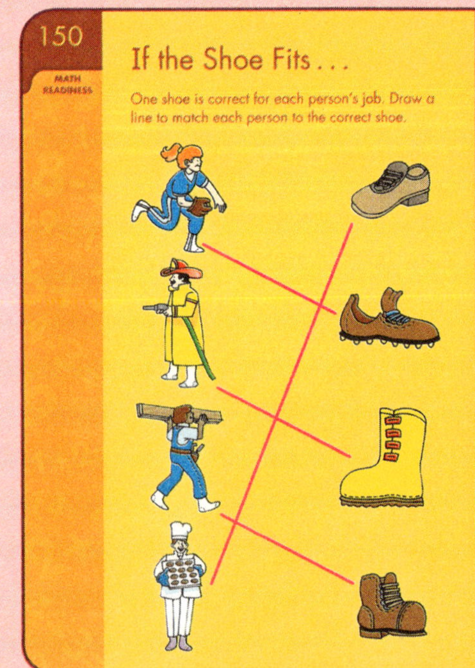
150
MATH READINESS
If the Shoe Fits . . .
One shoe is correct for each person's job. Draw a line to match each person to the correct shoe.

151
MATH READINESS
Dog Gone Home
Each dog needs a home. Draw a line to match each dog with a home.

152
MATH READINESS
Let's Count! 0
Trace and write the number **0**. Then, draw an **X** on the tanks with **zero** fish.
0 0 0
0 0 0

153
MATH READINESS
Zero 0
Trace and write the number word. Then, circle the number of fish in each tank.
zero
zero
0 1 3 0 1 2
3 4 5 0 1 2

154
MATH READINESS
Let's Count! 1,2
Trace and write the numbers **1** and **2**. Then, count and write the correct number.
1 1 1 1
2 2 2 2
1 2

155
MATH READINESS
One 1
Trace and write the number word. Then, circle each picture that shows **one** fruit.
one
one

156
MATH READINESS
Two 2
Trace and write the number word. Help the bunny twins catch their balloons. Follow the **twos** through the maze.
two
two

ANSWER KEY

157
MATH READINESS
One and Two
Count and write the number in each box. Circle the groups of one. Color the groups of two.
2
1
1
2

158
MATH READINESS
Let's Count! 3,4
Trace and write the numbers 3 and 4. Then, count and write the correct number.
3 3 3 3
4 4 4 4
3
4

159
MATH READINESS
Three 3
Trace and write the number word. Under each picture write the number of things.
three
three
3
1
3
2

160
MATH READINESS
Four 4
Trace and write the number word. Then, complete the picture by drawing four fish and four seagulls.
four
four
drawings will vary

161
MATH READINESS
Three and Four
Count and write the number in each box. Circle the groups of three. Color the groups of four.
4
3
4
3

162
MATH READINESS
Let's Count! 5
Trace and write the number 5. Then, color five dogs.
5 5 5
5 5 5

163 MATH READINESS

Five 5

Trace and write the number word. Write the correct number on each domino.

five

five

5 2 4 3 5 1

164 MATH READINESS

Review Numbers 1–5

Look at the picture. Read the questions. Circle the correct number.

How many in all? 1 2 3

How many in all? 1 2 3

How many in all? 2 3 4

165 MATH READINESS

Review Numbers 1–5

Look at the picture. Read the questions. Circle the correct number.

How many in all? 3 4 5

How many in all? 3 4 5

How many in all? 3 4 5

166 MATH READINESS

Let's Count! 6

Trace and write the number **6**. Then, draw **6** coins in the piggy bank.

6 6 6

6 6 6

167 MATH READINESS

Six 6

Trace and write the number word. Draw an **X** on each group of **six** things.

six

six

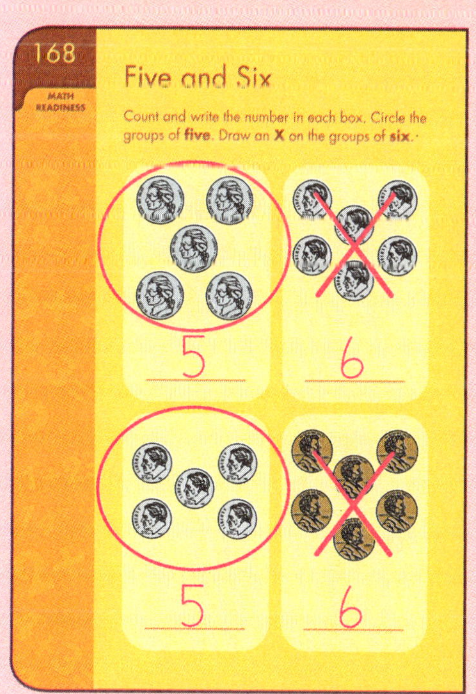

168 MATH READINESS

Five and Six

Count and write the number in each box. Circle the groups of **five**. Draw an **X** on the groups of **six**.

5 6

5 6

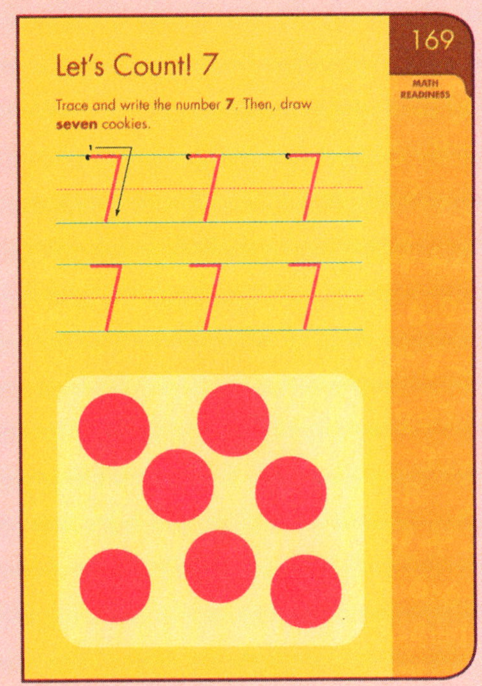
169
MATH READINESS
Let's Count! 7
Trace and write the number 7. Then, draw seven cookies.
7 7 7
7 7 7

170
MATH READINESS
Seven 7
Trace and write the number word. Count the ladybugs. Connect the dots. Color the picture.
seven
seven

171
MATH READINESS
Let's Count! 8
Trace and write the number 8. Then, draw eight peas on the plate.
8 8 8
8 8 8

172
MATH READINESS
Eight 8
Trace and write the number word. Color the pictures that have eight spots.
eight
eight

173
MATH READINESS
Seven and Eight
Count and write the number in each box. Circle the groups of seven. Color the groups of eight.
7
8
8
7

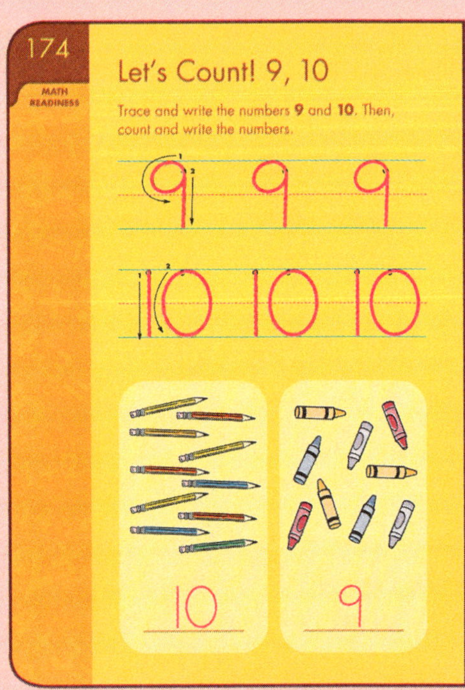
174
MATH READINESS
Let's Count! 9, 10
Trace and write the numbers 9 and 10. Then, count and write the numbers.
9 9 9
10 10 10
10
9

175
MATH READINESS
Nine 9
Trace and write the number word. Count the shapes on each quilt square below. Color the squares with **nine** shapes **green**. Color the other squares **yellow**.
nine
nine

176
MATH READINESS
Ten 10
Trace and write the number word. Write the numbers **1** to **10** on the empty hearts.
ten
ten
1 4 6 8 2 9 5 7 3 10

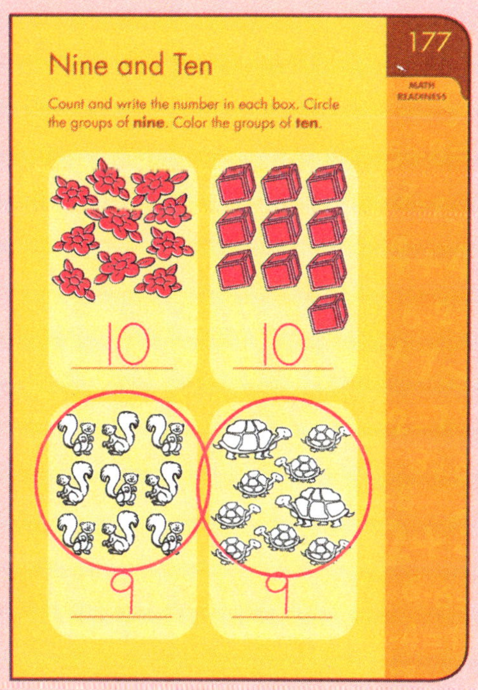
177
MATH READINESS
Nine and Ten
Count and write the number in each box. Circle the groups of **nine**. Color the groups of **ten**.
10 10
9 9

178
MATH READINESS
Review Numbers 1–10
Count the beads in each group. Write the number.
2
4
6
8
10

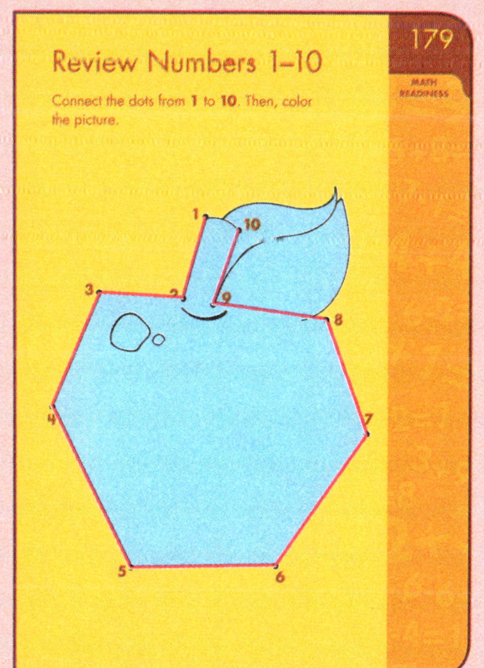
179
MATH READINESS
Review Numbers 1–10
Connect the dots from **1** to **10**. Then, color the picture.

180
MATH READINESS
Let's Count! 11, 12
Trace and write the numbers **11** and **12**. Then, count and write the numbers.
11 11 11
12 12 12
12 11

181 MATH READINESS

Eleven 11

Count Zeb Zebra's stripes and color them.

182 MATH READINESS

Twelve 12

Count each group of creatures. Draw a line from the creatures to their matching apples.

183 MATH READINESS

Thirteen 13

Trace and write the number **13**. Complete each puzzle by writing or drawing the missing number of flowers.

184 MATH READINESS

Fourteen 14

Trace and write the number **14**. Connect the dots. Color the picture.

185 MATH READINESS

Fifteen 15

Trace and write the number **15**. Write the missing pool ball numbers.

186 MATH READINESS

Sixteen 16

Trace and write the number **16**. Draw eight legs on each spider.

How many legs are there in all? 16

187
MATH READINESS
Seventeen 17
Trace and write the number 17. Circle each group of 17 things. Color the dog.

188
MATH READINESS
Eighteen 18
Trace and write the number 18. Help Filbert Fish find his way to the top. Write the numbers 1–18 in each bubble along the way.

189
MATH READINESS
Nineteen 19
Trace and write the number 19. Circle the numbers 1–19 in the picture.

190
MATH READINESS
Twenty 20
Trace and write the number 20. Connect the dots to find the hidden picture.

191
MATH READINESS
Time for Fun!
Trace the numbers 1–12 in order on the clock.
Hickory Dickory Dock,
The mouse ran up the clock.
The clock struck one and down he ran.
Hickory Dickory Dock.

192
MATH READINESS
Time Flies
Write the time that is on each clock.
2 o'clock
3 o'clock
9 o'clock
6 o'clock

193
MATH READINESS
Time Flies
Write the time that is on each clock.
10 o'clock
11 o'clock
7 o'clock
8 o'clock

194
MATH READINESS
Penny Power
A penny is worth 1¢. It is brown. Circle the correct amount of money in each row below.
Example:
1¢
2¢
3¢
1¢
2¢
3¢
5¢
6¢
7¢
7¢
8¢
9¢

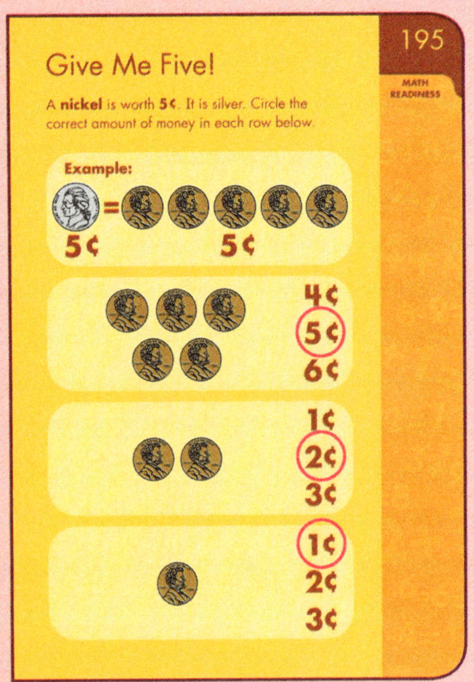
195
MATH READINESS
Give Me Five!
A nickel is worth 5¢. It is silver. Circle the correct amount of money in each row below.
Example:
5¢
5¢
4¢
5¢
6¢
1¢
2¢
3¢
1¢
2¢
3¢

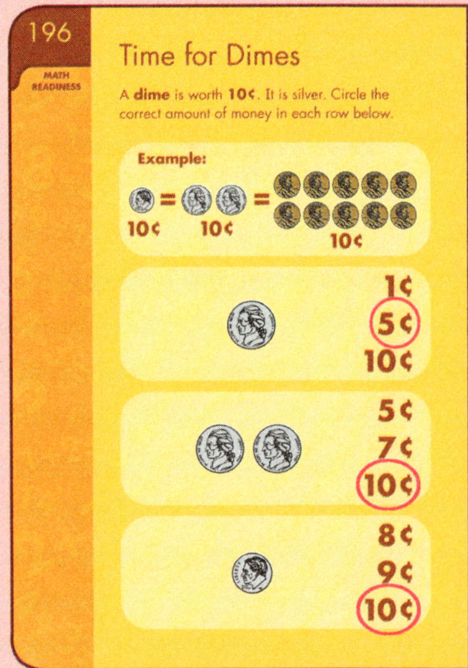
196
MATH READINESS
Time for Dimes
A dime is worth 10¢. It is silver. Circle the correct amount of money in each row below.
Example:
10¢
10¢
10¢
1¢
5¢
10¢
5¢
7¢
10¢
8¢
9¢
10¢

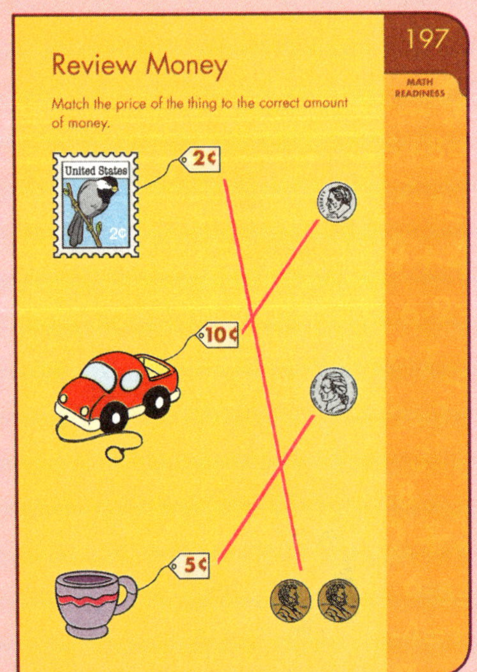
197
MATH READINESS
Review Money
Match the price of the thing to the correct amount of money.
United States
2¢
10¢
5¢

198
MATH READINESS
Review Money
Match the coins to the correct amount of money.
10¢
5¢
2¢
6¢
8¢
1¢

199
MATH READINESS
Get In Shape
Draw and color the shape that comes next in each pattern.

200
MATH READINESS
Get In Shape
Draw and color the shape that comes next in each pattern.

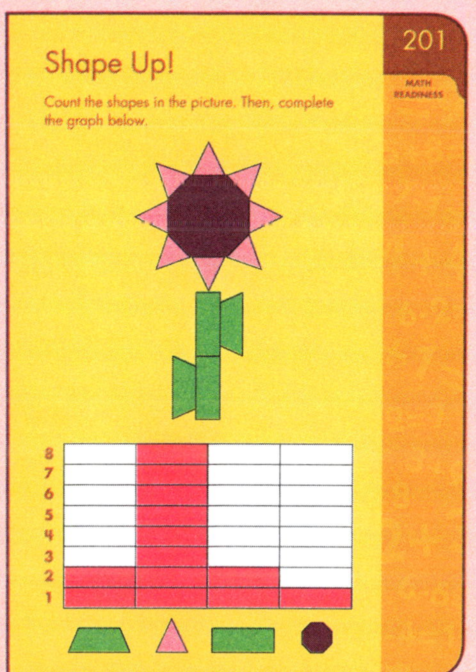
201
MATH READINESS
Shape Up!
Count the shapes in the picture. Then, complete the graph below.
8
7
6
5
4
3
2
1

202
MATH READINESS
Shape Up!
Look at the graph on page 201. Then, answer the questions below.
How many triangles are there? 8
How many rectangles are there? 2
How many octogons are there? 1
How many trapezoids are there? 2
Which two shapes are there the same number of?
rectangles and trapezoids
How many shapes are there all together? 13

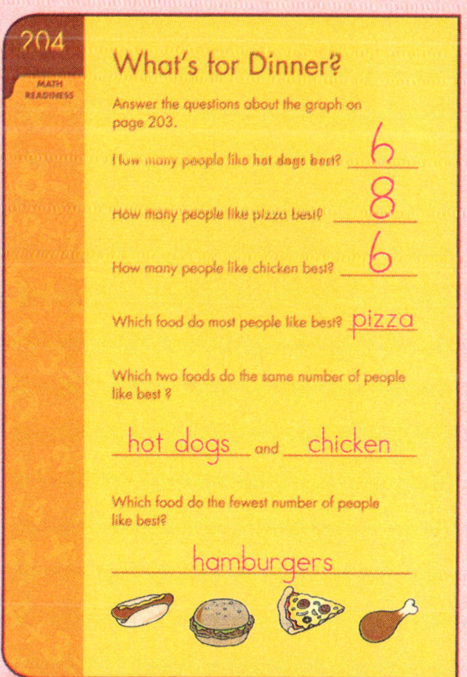
204
MATH READINESS
What's for Dinner?
Answer the questions about the graph on page 203.
How many people like hot dogs best? 6
How many people like pizza best? 8
How many people like chicken best? 6
Which food do most people like best? pizza
Which two foods do the same number of people like best ?
hot dogs and chicken
Which food do the fewest number of people like best?
hamburgers

205
MATH READINESS
Find Your Way Home
Read the clues below. Draw an X on the houses that do not fit the clues. Circle the correct house.
The house is white.
The house has a red door.
The house has a fence in front of it.

ANSWER KEY

206

MATH READINESS

Rain, Rain, Go Away

Read the clues below. Draw an **X** on the umbrellas that do not fit the clues. Circle the correct umbrella.

The umbrella is open.
The umbrella is big.
The umbrella has dots on it.

207

MATH READINESS

Going for a Ride

Read the clues below. Draw an **X** on the bicycles that do not fit the clues. Circle the correct bicycle.

The bicycle has a bell.
The bicycle is **blue**.
The bicycle has a flat tire.

208

MATH READINESS

Number Detective

Read the clues below. Draw an **X** on the numbers that do not fit the clues. Circle the correct number.

The number is **less** than **7**.
The number is **greater** than **2**.
The number **equals 3 + 1**.